She stood high on the ladder.

Faded blue jeans. Slim waist and long, shapely legs. David was intrigued. It had been a while since he'd seen a woman whose knees didn't tremble on the top rung of a ladder.

He stood, watching breathlessly. The surprise vision of the slender woman and the skill of her movements seen through the mist of exotic plants touched a chord within him that seemed to ring through to his heart.

David regretted the reason for his visit. What a shame—even if he could persuade her to accept some kind of compromise, the beautiful serenity of the garden and the house on the hill would be destroyed. He'd discussed the whole situation with his lawyer, the county development people and his own surveyors—there were no alternatives.

Dear Reader,

Welcome to Silhouette. Experience the magic of the wonderful world where two people fall in love. Meet heroines who will make you cheer for their happiness, and heroes (be they the boy next door or a handsome, mysterious stranger) who will win your heart. Silhouette Romances reflect the magic of love—sweeping you away with books that will make you laugh and cry, heartwarming, poignant stories that will move you time and time again.

In the next few months, we're publishing romances by many of your all-time favorites, such as Diana Palmer, Brittany Young, Emilie Richards and Arlene James. Your response to these authors and other authors of Silhouette Romances has served as a touchstone for us, and we're pleased to bring you more books with Silhouette's distinctive medley of charm, wit and—above all—*romance*.

I hope you enjoy this book and the many stories to come. Experience the magic!

Sincerely,

Tara Hughes
Senior Editor
Silhouette Books

JULI GREENE
Beneath a Summer Moon

Silhouette **Romance**

Published by Silhouette Books New York

America's Publisher of Contemporary Romance

SILHOUETTE BOOKS
300 E. 42nd St., New York, N.Y. 10017

ISBN: 0-373-08499-4

First Silhouette Books printing April 1987

America's Publisher of Contemporary Romance

Printed in the U.S.A.

JULI GREENE

a true globe-trotter, has traveled by train, ship, plane as well as by elephant, camel and donkey. She's been to five of the seven continents and seen such countries as South Africa, Morocco, Sudan, Italy, Spain and Greece—to name a few. She is proud of the collection of jewelry she's accumulated from her journeys and when she's not traveling with her husband, she enjoys her hobbies of cooking, riding and guitar playing—but of course her first love is writing.

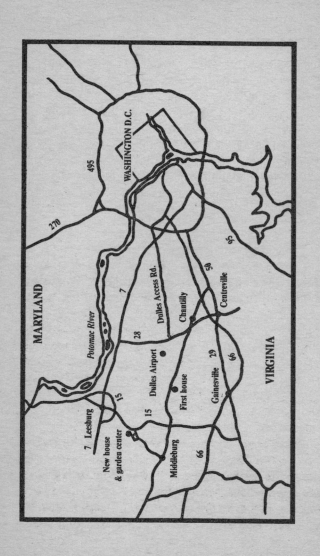

Chapter One

Early evening sun flooded the kitchen. Its fading light touched Janice Haley's winter-brown hair as she opened the oven door, slid out the middle shelf and checked on the casserole. In a gesture that had remained with her from childhood, she brushed a damp lock from her forehead with the back of her slim, capable hand, and then pushed the shelf back.

Not much longer, she thought wearily. Sometimes she wondered if being independent was worth all the extra work.

It had been a longer day than usual in the greenhouses. She felt as though she'd been indentured for life to the delicate greenery locked away from a hostile environment. Most of her plants originated in the tropics, and even the mildness of Washington area winters was deadly to them. All winter long she'd nursed, fed and cultivated them. With the coming of spring here, both the growing and the selling season were just around the corner, and all her time was spent manicuring the plants, repotting, propagating and pruning them. The new cuttings she'd taken from last year's stock were safely growing in their own peat pots. By the end of next month, they could be moved outside, where they'd spend the growing season under the sun.

She shook excess water off the lettuce and tossed it into the salad bowl. Homegrown was always better, she thought, looking proudly at the tender shoots of leaf lettuce and the early tomatoes and cucumbers from the greenhouse, but nothing could beat the taste of fresh vegetables grown outdoors under the open sky. How she loved the summer. Even now, this early, she could smell the new growth of the trees putting out buds.

Within a month, she thought as she leaned her elbows on the hand-painted tiled kitchen counter and gazed out at her two young sons, within a month the backyard would look entirely different. That horrible new town-house complex visible through the bare branches of the trees would disappear behind a rustling wall of intricately varied leaves and vines and bushes.

She smiled at the sight of Jason and Jonathan absorbed in their play. Their dark heads were close together. Jason, eight grown-up years already behind him, was holding forth on the engineering wonders involved in constructing the massive walls necessary to defend the integrity of the last bastion of civilization against the depredations of the evil empire. Jonathan, who still retained the slightly unformed edges of his babyhood, listened with rapt attention.

The younger boy stood up, sand running in crystalline rivulets down his old jeans. He ran across the lawn to the kitchen door. "Mom, I need a spoon!"

"Why do you need a spoon?"

"Jason's going to make cannonballs," the little boy said proudly.

Janice handed him an old spoon, and he raced back, carefully holding the spoon out in front of him. Jason took it with a smile and a graceful nod of his head that startled his mother. It looked so charmingly adult! They were growing almost as fast as the plants did these days.

She smiled wistfully as she watched the two little heads of curly black hair that were so like their father's. If only . . .

No, Janice shook her head resolutely and took down the dinner plates. If onlys just didn't work. She could not—no, she *would* not—allow the past to haunt the present . . .

The clock chimed. It was six. Time for the news. Janice automatically turned on the television and tuned in Channel Four. She set the table as she watched the local broadcast from the corner of her eye. As the newscaster's voice bantered on about the weather, Janice arranged the tomato wedges around the sides of the salad bowl. She poured lemon juice and oil over the crisp greens and seasoned it. The timer on the oven buzzed, and she checked the casserole. It looked ready. The chicken pieces were nicely browned and glazed with pineapple juice and soy sauce. Julienne strips of green peppers and chunks of pineapple garnished this favorite supper of her sons'. In a last-minute rush of activity, Janice called the children, overriding their objections, and hurried them into the bathroom to wash their hands.

"Hurry up, you two. Your dinner's going to be cold," she called.

"Coming." Jason's muffled voice urged his brother to get a move on. She heard mumbles from the bathroom as the water shut off, and the boys raced for their seats. Janice served the casserole and tossed the salad.

"And in Fairfax County, the Phillips development has run into a new, or should we say very old, snag...."

Janice looked up as she handed the boys their plates. They must be talking about that new development right down the road from her. She strained to hear the rest of the story, but just at that moment Jason and Jonathan began fighting over the last bread roll. As she diplomatically divided it into two equal parts, she caught one last glimpse of the man on the screen.

Then he vanished, but her mind retained his image. His smile, that gesture of strong, capable hands emphasizing his words, the raising of an eyebrow, the way he shook the hair from his forehead—it burned into her heart. She felt she could have been alone with him, that stranger who seemed to complete her. Janice's safe, secure world—the world that she'd built over the past two years on the foundations of what Jay had left her—splintered and rearranged itself. Suddenly all was new, complex, like a kaleidoscope. She found herself standing on a precipice. The pattern of her life was now a new configuration built from all the same parts, but its intricacies were fresh, new, infinitely subtle and daring.

It was just a glimpse of a young man, just an image on television, but suddenly she was conscious of her loneliness, the desolation of those two years without a touch of love, or a kiss. She caught her breath on what sounded suspiciously like a sob. But her whole body tingled with excitement. What had brought this on? Surely not just the momentary image of a handsome young man? She drew a shaky breath.

He wasn't that devastatingly handsome! It must have been his voice, which was rich and warm; or perhaps his direct eyes or that quick and friendly smile....

"Mommy," a wail startled her, breaking through her preoccupation with the man on the screen. "I dropped my fork, and Smoky's licking it."

That was that. The boys hadn't noticed her inattention, and she chased the cat away, got Jonathan another fork, had the usual running battle with the children over their spinach and rewarded them with a fresh piece of carrot cake. Finally she excused them from the table, and they rushed back to their fortress.

Still bemused by her reaction to the man on television, Janice absentmindedly cleared the table. Who could he have been? She had only seen him for a moment, but his image stayed with her. His smile had seemed so intimate. It hovered between her and her familiar kitchen with the persistence of a melody that catches the imagination and lingers, returning again and again.

The story had been about Riverbend Park, but for the life of her she couldn't remember a word. Something about the road and an old—no, a very old—snag. But still the image of the man haunted and distracted her.

Despite her most earnest attempts, she felt detached from her after-dinner chores even as she was doing them. In her mind's eye she saw again that compelling presence. She laughed a bit shakily. Well, after all, it *had* been two years since her husband had died. No other man, even for a moment, had caught her attention since then. She just didn't have time. Her life had settled into a round of business, children, garden and home.

Stunned, she sat down in the living room window seat. What was happening to her? She drew a deep breath and tried to regain control.

This was her favorite spot in the whole house. From here, she could see the old trees spreading their long shadows on the front lawn and the edges of the now darkened greenhouses extending from the side of the house. And through the back door she could see the top of the jungle gym and hear the children playing.

Jay had rarely joined her here in the evenings. All of his days and most his nights had been devoted to his medical practice. He'd always said that by the time he was forty he'd have a partner to share the work and that they'd be able to travel.

Dear Jay, he'd never made it to forty, never had the chance to travel with her.

Janice thought back to the first time she'd seen him. To her eyes he'd been genuinely handsome, with his short dark hair that insisted on curling even though he kept it at a military half inch, his Irish-blue eyes that sparked with intelligence and his tall, spare frame that looked rangy in his army uniform.

Jason Haley had come to Champaign/Urbana, Illinois, for a seminar in gastroenterology. Janice's mother, a doctor with both a private practice and a teaching post at the University of Illinois medical school, had been impressed by the young army doctor. Their technical discussion had continued long past the close of the workshop, and she had invited him home for dinner.

That evening, long after her parents had retired for the night, she and Jay had stayed up late talking about bone structure in modern man and in the most primitive skeletons just discovered, Janice's particular area of expertise.

It had been a whirlwind courtship. Jay had managed somehow to get to Central Illinois almost every weekend, and by the time she had graduated with a B.A. in English and Anthropology, their wedding date had been set, and her postgraduate plans left to wither, along with her girlhood ambitions.

Looking back on it now, Janice realized that she had gone from childhood to adulthood to motherhood within the space of one year. Before Jay, there had been no one—no boyfriends, no close girl-friends, no brothers or sisters. Janice's father had been a professor all of his adult life. He was currently head of the School of Business and Management, and Janice, as an only child, had been raised to enjoy adult conversation. Her parents had scared away any visitors just by being so successful and so intelligent. When visiting Janice meant sitting in the parlor trying to understand the subtleties of international trade deficits or the latest developments in treating liver infections, no one ever came around twice.

But Jay had fitted into that environment as though born to it. He'd take her out to dinner and dancing and then talk shop until dawn with her mother.

Janice shook her head, remembering. Her parents, in their gentle way, had encouraged her to wait, to finish her education, and then decide about her life. But a master's degree and teaching career had seemed unimportant in the face of Jay's ardor. Then the accident had come, which killed Jay's parents and bought Randy, Jay's teenage brother, to live with them. From that time on, the fledgling passion had never had a chance—not with her duties as a surrogate mother and Jay's driving ambition. Yet they'd had a good life.

It had never been overwhelmingly romantic. The whole situation had been so easy, so meant, that they had just slid into marriage, a home, a mortgage and a family without ever feeling the searing fires of passion. Janice had half expected the passion to develop, but it never had, and she hadn't felt deprived. Jay had left the army to start his own practice, and from that moment on he'd either been out working or at home exhausted. The children hadn't been planned, but were welcomed, and Janice's days had quickly filled with housework and taking care of the babies and her husband.

The accident that had killed Jay had brought that comfortable life to an abrupt end.

She realized with amazement that for the first time since his death she was thinking about him without that awful, wrenching pain at his loss.

The initial shock of losing him had been suppressed almost immediately by the need to continue, to make a normal life for the children. So many people had gathered around. Her mother had swept into the house, bringing a hard-headed realism with her that had no room for tears and tranquilizers. Her father had been the one who'd held her and comforted her those few times she'd broken down.

But the children and their loss had always been paramount. Perhaps, after all, it had been their need that had kept her going.

Her grief had taken a back seat to fixing the meals, making the beds and packing the lunches. And now, when at last she'd found herself remembering, the grief was practically gone—it had faded away unnoticed over the years.

Jay—she tried frantically to call up his smile, the touch of his hands. But she couldn't; it was all gone.

Janice buried her head in her hands, appalled at herself. Jay had been half of her life. Could only two years have been enough time to accept such a loss?

But he was truly gone. Sadly she raised her head. Fate had left her with the children and she'd had to continue on by putting his memory aside. Perhaps that was the way it had to be, she thought.

But now it bothered her that all she could visualize was a new face, that of a young stranger with straight dark hair and hazel eyes glimpsed only for a moment.

She twisted her wedding ring. Ten years—for ten years this ring had been a part of her. She looked over at Jay's picture on the wall. Even after his death, she now realized, he'd looked after them.

It had been his insurance that had given her what she'd needed to start the business. The house they'd bought together had become both a home and a nursery garden, and Elaine Creighton, an old friend, had become her partner and the manager of what was now a thriving business. She felt a momentary guilt, which she immediately fought. She'd done what she'd had to do. If that cost her the memory of her love for Jay, then that was the way it had to be.

Jonathan didn't remember his father at all, except from photographs, and Jason Junior's memories had faded into the realm of "once upon a time."

Even here in his home, she reflected sadly, Jay was visible only in the tangled curls of his son's and the old pictures in the album.

Perhaps it was better that way. If the pain had remained intense, she and the boys would never have been able to continue with the present.

The day faded slowly into darkness, and the boys came in from the garden, covered with sand and bits of grass.

Janice put down her cup. "Oh, look at you! What a mess." She herded them up the stairs and into the bathroom and ran the water for their baths.

"Oh, Mommy, we just had a bath yesterday."

"Yes, but you're dirty again today. Come on now, hop in."

Grumbling, Jason led the way into the tub, and by the time Janice slipped out the door, the boys were splashing each other and shrieking with laughter.

She went into their room, automatically clearing up the scattered toys and socks and turning down the beds. The long day in the greenhouses settled on her shoulders, pushing her into exhaustion, but her mind still worried at the scraps of information she'd caught on the news. Any change in the development plans could have a serious effect on both her home and her business. The road construction had been due to start last week, and it now occurred to her that she hadn't yet heard the bulldozers begin work. Could the news item have been about that?

That man she'd seen—his face rose again before her eyes—was he somehow connected to the development? And what was it about him that had so affected her?

"Mommy, Mommy." Two wet arms clutched round her knees, and a small head burrowed against her. "Jason took my towel." Her hand gently stroked her son's dark, wet curls.

"No, I didn't. That one's mine." Her elder son stood in the doorway, the Superman towel draped in toga fashion over his shoulders. "Jonathan's is the Hulk, and it got all wet. So there," he said triumphantly, sticking his tongue out at Jonathan.

For a moment Janice's tolerance was drowned by her exhaustion, but she collected herself as the argument began to escalate. "Stop that right now. Jason, go get the Spiderman towel for your brother. Jonathan, let go!"

Jason's mouth narrowed in rebellion, but one look at his mother's determined scowl sent him to the linen closet, somewhat slowly. Still frowning, he brought the dry towel for his brother. "Thank you, Jason," she said, taking his hand and holding it to her cheek. "I don't know what I'd do without you."

He grinned at her, temper gone. "Aw, Mom," he said in his grown-up voice, and gently pulled his hand away.

She smiled as she saw him surreptitiously stick his tongue out at his brother again. The constant rivalry between the two boys occasionally worried her. It was hard to know how to handle it, and her policy, decided through trial and error, was to reward kindness with kindness. Jason always pretended that he didn't like her "holding his hand," as he put it, but she knew the sign of affection never failed to please him.

Finally, the boys were settled for the night. As Janice wearily turned out the light and started downstairs, she could hear muted whispers as they tried to stave off sleep.

This was the time Janice spent making the final rounds of the greenhouses. Now, at this time of night, there was no one she had to pay attention to, no one to explain things to. She loved her children, but the constant effort of providing them with a stable, loving, understandable environment exhausted her. The greenhouses were her secret balm.

They had started out as one porch. On her twenty-fifth birthday, Jay had taken her to New York for the weekend, and on their return he had surprised her with the fait accompli—a fully equipped plant room. Janice had reveled in making it the most attractive room in the house. They had spent most of their time in that room. Much to her own surprise, Janice had discovered not only a love of plants, but a miraculous knack in caring for them. Within months, the room had become a veritable jungle. Jay had been a bit irritated; it turned out that his plans for the room had included a hot tub and a winter solar retreat, not solid greenery.

After his death, when Janice had begun to think of ways and means of supporting herself, Elaine had been the one to suggest starting a nursery. For years she had marveled at Janice's ability to grow things. The idea had taken root, and they had immediately added another, larger greenhouse off the porch room. Part of the front yard and the whole length of one side of the house had been turned into an outdoor nursery for the hardier plants.

Janice pulled open the door of the greenhouse and entered the warm, moist atmosphere. She walked slowly down the narrow, leafy aisles, checking the new buds, the thermostats and the humidity. She loved the scent of these rooms; the moist, earthy smell that permeated the air. At night, when all was quiet, it was the most private place in the world. She could walk through this tropical climate in perfect comfort, while outside the night was turning cold and crisp. She could allow her mind to wander into secret realms.

Ever since she was a child, Janice had fantasized about life on a tropical island. She'd dreamed of picking her lunch from exotic fruit trees growing wild, of living in a tree house with no roof, watching brilliant birds diving from branch to branch. Now she had her own little bit of the tropics. Could any island ever really have that fragile charm that she herself delighted in, here, so far from its natural setting? These greenhouses transcended the fantasy, and every leaf, flower and plant was so dear to her.

She turned out the lights and locked the door. With a sigh, she made her way upstairs, took a bath and leaned back against the pillows with an old yellowing copy of an Asey Mayo detective story. Her eyes kept drooping over the normally engrossing words. She shook her head. It was only 9:50. The news would be on in ten minutes. The very thought galvanized her. Throwing aside her book, she swung her long legs to the floor and eagerly switched on the television. The reception was as poor as usual, but rather than ignoring it she furiously manipulated the rabbit ears in an attempt to get rid of the ghost. She was only marginally successful. At least, she thought as she got back into bed, it could be worse. Any story about the Phillips development was sure to affect her, and if they reran the story, she should just be able to make out his features.

Janice pulled herself up. Drat that man—his face, his voice, his whole presence had haunted her all evening. Even now she could feel her heart quicken and her hands tremble slightly in anticipation.

Was the chance of seeing that man the main reason she wanted to catch the show again? Janice started to laugh quietly. All evening she'd been playing games with herself about this fellow. She'd even managed to fool herself into believing it was the story she was looking forward to—it was always handy to have an excuse. And in this instance, hearing the entire story of the changes in the development would serve perfectly.

She laughed at herself again as she rehearsed this train of logic in her mind. Why should she need an excuse? What was wrong with enjoying the sight of a sexy young man? It wasn't as though she was planning to go out and seduce the poor guy. Was she? She giggled uncertainly, picturing herself as a cradle-robbing seductress. He couldn't be all that much younger than she was, perhaps Randy's age. She blushed, thinking of herself chasing after one of Randy's friends. Oh, no, she couldn't do that!

But why not, she asked herself, her heart racing as the time grew closer. After all, Randy was a grown man, and the age difference between them was more in her mind than in reality. Randy was working as an executive engineer in Saudi Arabia. The true difference between herself and Randy was in their lifestyles. She was a business owner, settled, a single parent of two children, whereas Randy wasn't ready for the responsibility of a family yet. She grinned as she remembered the frenetic dating he'd packed into his last home leave.

What was that man on television like, she wondered idly as the minutes crawled by. Was he married? No! Instantly and automatically, Janice's thoughts rejected this notion. With that daredevil smile he had to be single, probably as much of a heartbreaker as her brother-in-law.

Janice felt suddenly embarrassed at her own thoughts. This obsession with a man seen for only seconds astonished her. Nothing like it had ever happened to her before. Not even—yes, she acknowledged to herself—not even when she'd first met Jay. She knew she was being ridiculous, but what did it matter? It couldn't do any harm, could it? She shrugged. It wasn't likely to ever make any difference in her life.

She turned her attention to the television and leaned back to indulge her foolishness, all the while wondering at herself.

What was it about him?

And then, there he was, talking in a deep, resonant voice about Indian burial grounds. She leaned forward, entranced by the sight of him. He had well-cut dark brown hair, hazel eyes, a firm mouth, broad forehead, strong chin. His build was tall and lean, with an understated power that showed even through his exquisitely tailored tweed suit. But it was none of his individual features that so moved her.

There was something, some indescribable quality about him that called to her—it blazed from his every movement, every nuance of his voice. An honest and genuine kindness, an enthusiasm in life itself came across so clearly that she felt herself respond involuntarily.

Then he was gone. Another man, an ordinary mortal, took his place on the screen.

At eleven o'clock, a bemused Janice realized that she'd entirely missed the story she'd set out to hear. She'd been mesmerized by a stranger's face on a screen.

She was none the wiser about the Indian burial site, about the development, about the weather. In fact, the only thing she could remember from the news report was that man, and she'd even missed hearing his name.

Chapter Two

The whole house shook faintly to the throbbing rumble of a big engine coming closer, louder, then fading, only to be replaced by yet another rumble.

Janice moaned and rolled over, burying her head under the blankets. Closing her eyes tightly, she tried desperately to retrieve the sleep from which she'd been so rudely snatched.

She'd been free, cherished, dancing effortlessly, held closely in the arms of...it was gone. The remnants of her dream faded too quickly. She was left clutching only the memory of a wonderful, secure feeling.

Could it be time to get up already? She peered at the alarm clock. It was only five! She groaned and burrowed deeper into the warmth of her bed. Scraps of her dream came back as she tried to deny the morning. She felt languorous, her body still responding to the dimly remembered caresses, the urgency of her dream partner's embrace.

Janice's eyes opened wide with shock. Now she was even dreaming about him! She sat up in bed. She really had to get hold of herself. It was one thing to daydream, another entirely to have a moment's television image wandering in and out of erotic dreams. Thank goodness dreams were still private! Janice wriggled down into the covers. She felt like a naughty schoolgirl reading the forbidden novel making the rounds of the dorm.

The rumble of heavy construction equipment was growing louder with each passing moment. Apparently the warm, drowsy feeling of being not quite awake was to be denied her this morning as it had been every morning since construction had begun.

Janice frowned. This area had been practically wilderness when she and Jay had moved here. Now the peace that she'd so enjoyed here had been shattered—would it ever be the same again? She feared it wouldn't, neither outside the house nor inside her own mind. This construction was only a symbol of change. It would leave behind a brand-new community and its four-lane highway. But more than just the landscape was changing. She herself felt restless, in need of change, dissatisfied with the quiet tenor of her life.

With a sudden chill, Janice realized her cocoon-like existence was gone—forever shattered by the eyes of a stranger.

Angry and confused, she gave up on her sleep. Throwing back the covers, she made for the shower, too irritated to do her regular exercises. The morning air was cold. As she dragged on a clean pair of jeans and a warm flannel shirt, she reflected wryly on the irony—romantic dreams of effortless dancing and jeans certainly didn't mix.

Sitting down at the antique dressing table she'd refinished the year Jason was born, she brushed her sleep-tangled hair. Her first few strokes were rough, in tune with her mood, but gradually the repetition calmed her, and she began to respond as she always did to the sheer sensuality in the smooth, soft stroking. In this light, she mused, it was hard to tell that she was already thirty-two. It was only up close that the small lines around her eyes and on her forehead were visible.

She peered closely at herself in the mirror. Her skin was clear, healthy, with a luminous golden tan, even this early in the year. There was a lot to be said, she thought, for an active outdoor life. In exchange for slightly work-roughened hands and a few extra wrinkles on her face, the work gave a glow to her skin and eyes. She cocked one eyebrow at herself as she stood up. She didn't look too bad, actually. Hard work in the garden kept her slim and supple. Even in her jeans the feminine curves of her trim, lithe figure were apparent. "You know why you're doing this?" she asked her image. "It's because of that man." She shook her head in exasperation at her continued obsession.

This was ridiculous. It was one thing to dream, quite another to allow her fantasies to influence her every thought, every movement, every action. But the loneliness of the past two years looked back at her from the mirror, and she quailed at the sudden thought of spending the rest of her life alone.

It was true. She was alone. She was a widow. She had two sons. They, as long as they were dependent upon her, had to be her top priority.

Reluctantly but firmly putting her daydreams aside, she laid her hairbrush down, put on her sneakers and left the room. As she tiptoed past their bedroom, she peeked in at the boys.

How she envied them in their continued slumber. By rights, she shouldn't have to get up for another hour and a half, but she'd never been able to sleep through the kind of din the boys could. Even as babies their sleep had been unshakable. Dogs howling, cats romancing—nothing disturbed them. She'd appreciated this gift when they had been infants, but now—it just wasn't fair—even the faintest of telephone rings brought her wide awake in the middle of the night.

Downstairs, she started the coffee, then puttered around the kitchen, taking out Jason and Jonathan's favorite cereal. As the coffee was brewing, she skimmed through the morning paper. The racket, the smell, the sheer overwhelming sight of the caravan of heavy equipment out front had grown to the point where she was driven from her usual window seat. She took refuge with her mug on the back patio.

Here at least she could hear the birds and pretend the world was still right.

It was chilly, the sun barely having risen, but she huddled contentedly in her sweater, breathing in the fragrant spring air. Coffee mug held close to her chest for warmth, she drew up her knees and listened to the cardinal's early song. The trees, the ground, the sky, everywhere there were birds and squirrels. The house provided enough insulation to dim the sounds of the heavy machinery on the road, and Janice enjoyed the relative peace until she could no longer sit still. It was too cold to be outside without being active, and Janice was not yet ready to begin the day.

She moved back inside to her window seat and sat cross-legged, looking out upon all the activity. Reluctantly fascinated, she watched as the enormous construction equipment rolled by, carrying assorted trusses and loads of brick and lumber. Two concrete mixers passed, followed by bulldozers on massive flatbed trucks. Almost lost among the gargantuan machines, a Jeep went by slowly in their dusty wake.

Dimly the alarm sounded in her bedroom. She'd forgotten to turn it off when she'd got up early. It was now officially time to get up—seven o'clock. Janice took her empty mug into the kitchen and filled it. It wasn't often that she had time for a second cup of coffee before she had to wake the boys, and she meant to enjoy every last minute of it.

Fifteen minutes later she went upstairs, smoothed Jason's hair from his face and kissed his forehead. "Breakfast is ready, Jase."

He always woke instantly. Sitting up, he smiled and swung his legs over the edge of the bed. "Morning, Mom."

She turned her attention to her younger son. Jonathan was more like her. He loved those last minutes in his warm bed, hanging on to the wispy ends of dreams. By the time Jason was awake and dressing, Jonathan was just sitting up, rubbing his eyes. "Come on, lazybones. Get moving," she prodded, leaning over to kiss him good morning. Two little arms reached up to clasp her neck, and she felt two dry little lips brush her cheek.

Once she was sure they were both up and moving, Janice went back downstairs. She chopped a couple of bananas into their bowls, put out the milk and poured the orange juice, listening all the time to the creaks of the old house under their quick bare feet. "Jason, Jonathan, you're going to be late," she called up the stairs. And at last they clattered down, tucking in last-minute shirttails. They gulped down their cereal and orange juice and grabbed their books on the way out the door.

Despairingly Janice wondered if mornings in the Haley home would ever be anything other than this same frenetic swirl of last-minute activity. Calling goodbyes, Jason leading, the boys bolted out the door and down the driveway just as the bus came into sight. Janice gave a sigh of relief. One more school day down, and just a few thousand left to go, she thought, grinning to herself.

Elaine arrived as the school bus pulled away. She called out and waved cheerily at the retreating children, but when she turned to Janice she was wearing what Janice always thought of as her "hardheaded businesswoman's" look.

Janice's partner, Elaine Creighton, was a striking woman in her mid-forties. There was about her, Janice thought admiringly, a sense of such self-assuredness that whenever Janice tried to picture her as a child, the best she could do was to visualize the modern-day Elaine shrunk magically to a height of three feet. She could never make herself believe in an Elaine with grubby knees, tear-streaked face or tangled hair.

As Janice looked affectionately at this amazing woman, she wondered for the hundredth time why Elaine had chosen to throw away her seniority and secure, well-paying job to embark upon such a chancy enterprise as E & J Garden Center. Elaine always said, with a quiet laugh, that she'd just been bored—ready for a change. But Janice secretly thought that it was the feeling of belonging to a family and being with the children that had brought Elaine to make such a choice.

Elaine was always well-groomed and well-dressed, preferring by choice the suit-and-vest look of professional women. With short styled hair and sharp features in direct contrast to an amazingly sensuous mouth, she was very striking. Janice always wondered why she'd never married. It wasn't as if she never had dates—indeed, she was very popular and led an active social life.

Whenever she asked, Elaine said simply that she liked her life the way it was, but Janice found herself unable to imagine wanting to live alone.

As she came up the steps, she took Janice's elbow and asked indignantly, "Did you see the news last night? Those creeps! They're going to put us out of business."

Janice's eyes widened. "What do you mean?" The news? She tried to gather her scattered thoughts together. "That old Indian burial ground?" It was all she could remember except for *him*.

"Of course, the old Indian burial ground!" Elaine mimicked. She peered curiously at her friend. "I thought you always listened to the local news. They showed the story at six and at ten." She shook her head impatiently. "They found it right where they were going to put the other two lanes of the highway."

"So?"

"So they'll most likely have to build on *our* side of the road. Which means cutting off the front of your yard for their highway. And what's that going to do to our plants—having traffic roaring past so close all day?" Elaine stormed indignantly into their office.

"No, they can't do that! Why don't you give the county a call and find out what their plans really are?"

"I'll just do that," Elaine's voice came from the other room.

As she dialed, Janice tried desperately to recall the news show. It was no use. She shook her head. She really couldn't remember anything about the story.

She fidgeted with the coffee, pouring Elaine's morning cup and another for herself.

"Drat!" Elaine exclaimed, taking the cup of coffee from Janice. "They're not open yet."

"Well, look," Janice said, "there's no need for us to get upset yet. We don't even know for sure what's happening. We'll wait until we've talked to the county people before we get all geared up to fight." Their eyes met, and she grinned at her friend's indignant look.

"If you think I'm upset now," Elaine said, "wait till they try to take down those trees out front. I've never believed in passive resistance." She put on a determined look.

They both broke out laughing and went into the office to review the day's orders. Even though the greenhouses kept plants thriving all year round, it was in the spring that people seemed to get around to buying new plants.

The people who had originally built the house would have been appalled at the use that their living and dining rooms were now being put to. When converting the house for business use, Janice had closed those two rooms off from the rest. The living room walls were lined with shelves stacked with weed killers, plant food, seeds and bulbs. The lovely old oak floor was scratched from heavy cartons of pottery and clay planters. Originally a large airy room, it now looked like a miniature warehouse, with small aisles winding between stacks of garden equipment piled almost to the ceiling in preparation for spring sales, and a checkout counter overlooking the new entrance, which had once been a tall, narrow window.

At the other end of the room, a newly hung utilitarian door was all that was left of the graceful arch that had divided the dining room from the front room. It led to a small and cluttered office.

The two partners' individuality was nowhere more apparent than in this room.

Elaine's desk was a modern miracle of organized space, with smoke-colored Lucite in and out trays, pen and paper-clip holders, a clean green blotter and a drawer neatly arranged with hanging file folders and typed labels. Janice's desk, on the other hand, was a battered relic from the days when her husband's younger brother had lived with them. Every visible surface was carved into intricate and intimate initials, doodles and one or two truly remarkable pieces of schoolboy scrollwork.

The walls of the office were lined with filing cabinets, and in the little space remaining, Janice had hung her favorite old etchings of squirrels, flowers and birds.

Most of these pictures had come with her from her childhood days in Illinois and had spent the years of her marriage in an old footlocker hidden away in the attic—Jay's taste had run more to an extravagant but rather gloomy collection of wall hangings.

Jammed in behind the doorway was Elaine's latest pride and joy—a small personal computer. Janice kept her distance from this miracle of modern technology. Despite Elaine's scoffing, Janice was convinced that it would self-destruct the moment she touched it.

They were mapping out the day's deliveries when the bell on the shop door sounded.

Elaine sighed with frustration. "Already!" She exited from the computer program and rose to deal with the early-bird customer.

Janice grinned behind Elaine's back. She knew Elaine loved to deal with people. Their partnership was the perfect match of complementary personalities.

They had met quite by accident at the local supermarket shortly after Janice and her husband had bought their house. They'd both reached for the last pint of strawberries at the same time. Janice had immediately retreated, and Elaine had grabbed them triumphantly. They'd laughed together, had coffee and talked for hours while the groceries had grown warm in the sun-drenched cars. That night, while Janice was serving dinner, the phone had rung. It was Elaine, laughing. The infamous strawberries had softened and fermented in the heat, and she'd tossed them out.

Their friendship had grown steadily from that time onward. After Jay's death, Elaine had been a prime mover in starting the nursery, giving up her career in accounting in favor of being her own boss. When setting up the business, they'd divided responsibilities—Janice took care of the plants and landscaping design, and Elaine handled the business end. Randy, her young brother-in-law, had even bullied her into taking several horticulture classes.

"Janice!" Elaine called from the shop. She was standing by the counter, tensely confronting two tired-looking men who were wearing suits and ties.

Janice went over to her.

"Mr. Davis and Mr. Pucchio here are from the County Planning Commission. They're going to run their road right through our nursery!"

The two women looked at each other, horrified.

"They can't do that!"

"Sorry, Mrs. Haley. We *can* do that, and we actually have no choice." Mr. Davis was apologetic but firm. "We have to widen this road, and the discovery of the burial grounds makes this our only alternative. The county will, of course, offer compensation for the property."

Elaine took a deep breath. "Let's sit down and discuss this." She unlocked the door leading into Janice's living room, and the two men reluctantly followed her.

An hour later, when they left, Elaine was sputtering with fury, and Janice sat bleakly in her window seat. It was a disaster. They would have to move the business, and she would have to find another home for herself and the children. These days the only thing they would be able to afford from the meager payment the county offered would put them much farther from the city and their regular customers. It had taken two years to build up the business.

She blinked away tears. Two long, hard years of work—to be started all over again. And what about the boys? They had been born in this house. All of her married life had been spent in this house. If she had to leave here, she would truly lose all touch with the past.

She looked around the room. The house had not been exactly what they'd wanted, but she and Jay had turned it into a comfortable, loved home. This window, she thought, running her fingers over the small panes of glass, he'd put this in especially for her on their fifth wedding anniversary.

Elaine's voice preceded her into the room. "Well, do you believe that? Of all the nerve! What are we supposed to do? And only giving us a month!" She looked around helplessly. "Dammit! I'm not going to let them get away with that!"

"What can we do?" Janice asked, her voice trembling.

"First of all, I'll call Mr. Hanrahan. He's our lawyer. This is what we pay him for." She came over and patted Janice awkwardly on the shoulder. "Don't worry. We'll come up with something."

Janice watched almost resentfully as Elaine swept briskly from the room. Don't worry, she thought, grimacing. Sure, they'd be able to find another place for the business, even if it cost more. But what about her home? She wandered disconsolately into the kitchen, leaned her elbows on the counter and looked out the back window. The children's sandbox and jungle gym, her grandfather's wren house that never failed to attract the small, magnificent singers, the irises she'd brought from her mother's house, the basketball net Jay had put up for his brother—all of these things would either be uprooted or disappear forever.

Elaine came up behind her and put an arm around her shoulders as she stood miserably contemplating the loss of all those years of memories. "Well, Mr. Hanrahan thinks he can get an injunction to stop work until we go to court. But he doesn't think it'll do us any good." She sounded tired and depressed—closer to tears then Janice had ever before seen her. "Oh, Janice, I'm so sorry."

Chapter Three

David Lee Phillips pulled his sleek silver-gray sports car into the dirt parking lot of the E & J Garden Center. Resting his hands on the steering wheel, he looked around. The place was a surprise. His meeting yesterday with the lawyer had led him to expect something much larger, perhaps a franchise, or at least an operation with a slicker, more commercial appearance. This small, charming site seemed almost too cozy for the fuss that it was causing. How on earth did that Madison Avenue type lawyer ever come to represent a business that had all the appearance of a little neighborhood mom-and-pop store?

He shook his head. When would it all end? A week ago it had been the uncovering of the Indian burial ground. How a few old bones, a few pottery shards and some arrowheads could bring a major construction project to a dead halt continued to amaze him. At first he'd been as excited as the archaeological team, thinking that the site would be an additional attraction for the park that he'd planned to have running along that side of the highway. However, the impossibility of running the highway around the other side of the burial ground due to unsuitable terrain and the piles of red tape necessary for the county to begin researching other options had become increasingly frustrating and irritating. At this point, just one week after the uncovering of the initial stumbling block, the entire construction schedule of Riverbend Park was in jeopardy. Every minute, every hour, every day lost brought closer the threat of massive new outlays of capital.

Then Mr. Pucchio of the County Planning Commission had called him with the bad news about the injunction. The entire road-building project was at a standstill until further notice all because one widow was concerned about her plants—at least that was the way Mr. Pucchio had told it.

David had immediately called upon his lawyer to meet with their lawyer. The report he'd received had been anything but encouraging. Mr. Hanrahan, representing E & J Garden Center, had all the papers, all the legal precedents, all the answers to any possible compromise David's lawyer had suggested. This project was causing him infinitely more trouble than he'd ever expected.

Never one to sit around waiting for events to unfold, David had made up his mind to speak directly to the owners of the garden center. He realized that

the widow had a point. Her business would have to
be moved, and that was always tricky.

Whatever Mr. Pucchio's feelings, David had to
admire the speed with which she and her partner had
slapped the injunction on them. If it went to court,
it could drag on for months, maybe even years,
turning Riverbend Park into a white elephant. By the
time the whole mess was decided, the entire concept
of the community he was trying to create might be
lost. Time was of the essence, not only to the development and the contracts, which could not stand for
that kind of delay, but also to the entire vision David was impatient to see fully realized.

Well, he thought to himself, staring through his
dusty windshield at the white clapboard house and
attached greenhouses, it was always better to talk
problems over face-to-face. And even though Mr.
Pucchio held out no hope of success—saying that
one partner was really hard-nosed—it certainly
couldn't do any harm.

David wrenched his thoughts away from the
problem, and his eyes focused on the scene before
him. It was, indeed, a charming little business. The
hand-painted sign pointing up the gravel driveway
was primitive in design but brightly colored and
beautifully executed. Brilliant birds and flowers
bordered the stark lettering. Pink and white dogwoods in full flower shaded the driveway, framing
the old white house. The parking lot was spotted with
old shade trees. And a new, immature border of
azaleas lined the perimeter of the whole lot.

Lovely. The landscaping was imaginative, showing a care that he appreciated greatly. The house and greenhouses were neatly set on the side of one of the small, rolling hills that made northern Virginia so beautiful.

David felt a growing appreciation of the setting as he looked around. The more he saw the more he liked it. In all of his own developments he'd tried to preserve the character of the existing environment, and even blend the new constructions into the landscape already there. The widow and her partner had obviously done exactly that with their property, and very successfully, too. Some of the tension he'd anticipated from the coming confrontation left him.

There must be a way he could come to some agreement with them. After all, they obviously shared a love of nature and an appreciation of beauty. Surely anyone able to see nature in this way would be able to sympathize with his own cherished idea for Riverbend Park and the danger it now faced.

Feeling decidedly more optimistic, he approached the house. A fresh, earthy scent of recently watered plants and soil filtered from the two greenhouses. Their different styles told him they had obviously been added at different times. The original must have been intended as a solar room, since it was part of the house. What had originally been a large side porch had been very carefully converted. The workmanship was impressive. The much larger attached structure was both more conventional and more utilitarian. David had no doubt, looking at this second greenhouse, that it had been especially designed for commercial use. It was newer and cheaper than the original but held at least four times as much. Through the misted glass, he could see hints of luxuriant growth pressed against the steamed-up sides.

David regretted the reason for his visit. What a shame. Even if he could persuade the two ladies to accept some kind of compromise, all of this would be destroyed. He could understand better now how upset they must be. If someone tried to take this from him, he knew he'd be furious. Even if they relocated to another spot just as lovely, the quiet beauty of their garden and the serenity of this house on the hill would be lost.

Impatiently David realized that Mr. Pucchio apparently didn't have the empathy to see what they would be losing. If only there were another way...

But there wasn't.

David had discussed the whole situation with his lawyer, the county development people and his own surveyors—there were literally no alternatives.

A bell announced his arrival as he opened the shop door. Even though he made his living designing new homes and offices, his first love had always been reserved for these old high-ceilinged farmhouses.

Through the glass enclosure of the old porch, he saw a flash of colorful movement among the plants and walked over to the glass separating the greenhouse from the store. The glass was still fogged over from the morning chill, and David futilely wiped at the mist, trying to see clearly through the damp tropical greenery.

Long legs high on a ladder. Faded blue jeans. Slim waist and rounded, feminine derriere. David was intrigued. It had been a long time since he'd seen a woman whose knees didn't tremble on the top rung of a ladder. He watched as slender, strong hands lifted a pane of glass and fitted it into its frame with skilled, sure movements. One hand held the pane in place, and the slim body bent, twisting around, showing a tantalizing outline of a young, shapely figure molded by a brown-and-blue flannel shirt, its sleeves rolled up above the elbows. She straightened and braced the pane in place at all four corners with a hammer.

He watched breathlessly. The surprise vision of the slender woman and the skill of her movements seen through the mist of exotic plants touched a chord within him that seemed to ring through to his heart. After what seemed a timeless moment, she expertly applied and smoothed the putty along the edges of the glass.

Her shoulder-length brown hair—wren-colored, he decided with delight—gleamed in the diffuse morning light, brushing seductively against her arms as they reached, flexed, stretched with her work.

"Excuse me."

David's attention snapped back to his surroundings. He was pressed to the glass enclosing the greenhouse, his hands framing his face, his breath misting the window. He turned abruptly, embarrassed, and cleared his throat. He was face-to-face with a woman wearing an immaculately tailored suit. She was trying unsuccessfully to hide a smile.

"May I help you?" Her voice was brisk but surprisingly sympathetic.

He cleared his throat again. Oh, no, he thought. This must be the hard-nosed partner. Gathering his aplomb, he searched her face, but the smile that he thought he'd seen was no longer in evidence. Damn Mr. Pucchio anyway. David didn't like being surprised in business. He usually reserved judgment until he could make his own, but here he had unconsciously accepted the prejudices of someone he didn't even know. The woman facing him and the entire nursery operation were competent and far from negligible. He immediately scrapped all of the half-hearted ideas he had brought with him and stepped forward, extending his hand.

"Yes. Thank you. My name is David Phillips."

Her face changed, hardened. "Mr. Phillips," she said brusquely, shaking his hand, "I'm Elaine Creighton. What can I do for you?"

David purposefully matched her businesslike manner, masking his racing thoughts with a bland, polite smile. "Ms. Creighton, I'm sorry to intrude, but it has always been my policy to discuss problems face-to-face. You've slapped me with an injunction halting work on the highway. I need that highway." He hesitated in the face of her granite glare, then plunged ahead. "I'm hoping we can talk this over without going through legal channels. There must be some solution that will be acceptable to both of us, and the only way we'll find it is to talk."

The hostility David sensed in Elaine abated somewhat as she looked at him skeptically, her eyes narrowed in assessment. She seemed to come to a decision, then abruptly walked past him and opened the door into the greenhouse. "Janice. Are you free? Can you come in here for a moment?"

A muffled reply filtered through from the greenhouse.

Elaine turned back to him. "My partner, Mrs. Haley, needs to be present if we are going to discuss business. This *is* her home, you know, as well as the E & J Garden Center."

David was startled. Those legs, that strong, sure competence he'd glimpsed through the glass—this was Mr. Pucchio's widow? His hope of coming to an understanding was foundering on misinformation. And this was the first he'd heard that the site involved both home and business, although he should have suspected something of the sort as he came up the driveway. His bad temper of the morning threatened to return as he stifled an exclamation, but then the humor of the morning's misconceptions hit him, and he shook his head in frustration. At least, he thought, remembering the view through the misted glass, the morning hadn't been a total loss. He began to look forward to meeting the possessor of those long, supple legs.

Ms. Creighton led the way through the aisles of gardening materials and unlocked a door behind the counter. "Let's go into the living room. Our office is a bit small for a meeting."

Her words reminded him once again of his problem, and as he followed her into a charming, airy room, he was furiously cursing Mr. Pucchio and trying desperately to come to grips with the changed situation. That stupid man—why hadn't he given any indication that this was a home as well as a business? Dammit, this was a whole new ball game. Of course the county wouldn't have offered them enough to compensate for losing both home and business! His mind worried at the problem as he allowed himself to be seated in a wicker armchair. Despite its insubstantial looks, it was surprisingly comfortable. It was turned slightly, facing a large bay window, looking out across the front lawn to the trees bordering the parking lot. The lush green view didn't make his position easier. He wished ...

The door opened, and David rose eagerly to greet Mrs. Haley.

The jeans and flannel shirt proclaimed that it was indeed the woman he'd seen, but the work clothes hadn't prepared him for the woman in them. She moved with a smooth, feminine grace, the rough clothes looking almost elegant on her. Her eyes focused on him.

"Mr. Phillips," he heard Elaine say, "this is my partner, Mrs. Janice Haley."

Janice, David thought as he came forward in a daze, murmuring what he hoped were the traditional polite phrases, and taking her hand. The formality, usually so mundane, took on a new significance at the touch of her slender, strong fingers against his palm. He puzzled light-headedly at the feelings churning through him as Elaine continued.

"Janice, this is Mr. David Phillips. He's the developer of Riverbend Park..."

Janice knew that Elaine was speaking to her, but she didn't hear a word. The shock of seeing before her in the flesh the man who'd haunted her dreams for the past week and reawakened emotions that she'd almost forgotten was so great that she felt separated from the reality of herself, her living room and Elaine's continuing voice. If the earth had opened up and swallowed her, she would have been grateful. She struggled to breathe.

In person, he was devastating. The room seemed smaller around him, and yet at the same time larger, in the sense that she was no longer aware of anything else. If she looked directly at anything, he was a part of it; his presence pervaded her senses. Whatever magic it was that she'd sensed in that first small glimpse of him a week ago filled the room and pierced her very heart.

David stood awkwardly, his initial curiosity suddenly transformed into something he couldn't name. Her eyes—deep brown, rich, gentle and alive—seemed to look deeply into him, into his very soul, awakening a passion that threatened to overwhelm him.

"...and has come to try to work things out..." Elaine's voice seemed a whisper in the background.

His hair was dark brown and straight, rich, silken, gleaming in the light from the window, and her fingers longed to touch it, rumple it, taste its thickness. His eyes were those magical kind whose color changed to fit time, place and mood. They were framed by thick, dark lashes, and she caught tantalizing glimpses of gray, green and sun-drenched brown. When they met hers, it was as though the whole world had stilled for just a moment.

She wore no makeup, her skin as smooth, as pure, as fresh as a flower, and she was lovely with a slender, feminine grace. Her mouth was perfect, but the shadow of a quiver trembled across its tender outlines, and he yearned to rouse her, to waken her to passion, driving the vulnerability away from those wide, inviting lips.

"... although he hasn't yet said..."

She couldn't look at him anymore. She turned her eyes away, quailing before the strength of her reaction to him.

Mercifully she released him, turning her eyes away, and he was able to draw breath again.

"... what specific measures he has in mind." Elaine stopped. Neither of them had heard a word she'd said. She looked from one to the other, aware of the tension that crackled in the air between them. She shook her head, intrigued and puzzled at the same time. "Janice, do you think we could have coffee?" Her eyes narrowed as she watched David watch Janice.

"Oh, yes. Just a moment... I'll get some." She hesitated, then walked from the room, her back tense with the knowledge of his eyes on her.

David only managed to wrench his gaze from Janice as she disappeared through the door. He turned to Elaine, who was busy pulling up another chair and a small table. "Let me help you." He sounded unnatural even to himself.

"I've got it."

Her voice stabilized him. She was so brisk, so casual, so normal. He felt his heartbeat begin to settle into a more regular rhythm. He sat down.

By the time Janice came back into the room, he was once more in command of himself.

Janice was proud of her composure. Not a rattle, not a spill—the tray of coffee and cups gave not a hint of her response to his presence.

She poured.

As she placed the cup into his hands, he murmured, "Thank you."

Even lowered, his voice was resonant and rich, and as his hand brushed hers it sent a shock right up her arm. She glanced at him. Had he felt that? But his face was impassive, his eyes politely fixed on Elaine.

"Now," Elaine said pointedly, "what did you have in mind?"

What did he have in mind? David collected himself, leaning back in his chair with careful nonchalance. "Firstly," David said, drawing the word out, his mind racing, "I had no idea that your business was also a home. That changes everything."

"How so?" Elaine asked.

"I had thought to offer you a more equitable price—one that would allow you to find suitable business premises. But now I realize that you will need to find both a business and a private property."

Elaine nodded emphatically in agreement.

"Another point..." He looked at Janice. "It appears that you grow your own plants both inside and out. That means that any business site you buy will have to come with additional land. Is that correct?"

Janice nodded, not trusting herself to speak.

He looked back at Elaine.

"Perhaps we can work out an extra sum to compensate you for the short notice..." He stopped.

Elaine was shaking her head. "That won't be sufficient. We have two properties, even though they *are* occupying the same site. And thirty days in which to find *two* new places is just impossible."

And the battle began.

Elaine and David talked and talked. Janice, feeling still dazed by her encounter with him, her nerves still reacting to his presence, made some more coffee and tended the store, absolutely unable to follow the intricate windings of their logic. Thankfully it was a slow day, and she had time to begin the horrendous process of inventorying every item—down to the last packet of seeds—in preparation for the move. She heard bits and pieces of their conversation as she moved through the room.

Still stunned at her reaction to him, she couldn't bear to sit there so close to him pretending polite uninvolvement. And the very thought of negotiating with him, pressing for advantage—she knew she couldn't do it.

"So we are agreed?" she heard him ask at last. "Payment for two properties?"

Elaine's voice had softened considerably; she was bringing her formidable feminine charm to bear now that the negotiations were in their final stages.

"We're still left with the problem of having to be out of here in thirty days," Janice heard her say. "And it's going to be impossible to remain open for the entire time—that's assuming, of course, that we can find a suitable property within the next two weeks."

"Well..."

"And do you have any idea," she pressed on, "how difficult it will be to move three thousand plants?"

David had no answer to that. Facing this tough opponent in the guise of a trim, attractive, middle-aged woman, he realized that the difficulties of moving a business such as a plant nursery had simply not occurred to him. Now that Elaine had pointed it out, he began to realize that even those plants and trees he'd found so charming around the parking area would either have to be moved or abandoned.

"Do you have any suggestions?" He was at a loss. "Perhaps—" he shook his head helplessly "—perhaps my company could help move them. I have the trucks and could spare some workers for a time."

Janice came back into the room to see them both apparently at a loss. She hesitated. Should she join in? Just as she was gathering her nerve to speak, Elaine's expression changed. It took on that eager, aggressive, on-the-hunt look Janice had come to recognize. What was Elaine up to?

Janice quickly retreated to the store and plunged back into the inventory. Inventory—she returned the handmade ceramic pot to the shelf. That was one more item listed. She brushed the hair from her forehead with a dusty hand and looked around her in dismay. Still so much to do and so little time in which to do it.

She glanced at the closed doors leading to the living room. What could be going on in there? It had been more than an hour. Every once in a while she could hear faint voices, but no individual words.

Well, knowing Elaine, something must be getting accomplished. Otherwise Mr. Phillips—she found herself reluctant to even think of him as David— would have been ushered out within minutes, since Elaine never wasted her time on lost causes.

Just then the door opened. Janice quickly glanced over at them. Elaine looked like the cat who'd stolen the cream. All smiles, eminently satisfied, she winked at Janice from behind Mr. Phillips's back.

Janice turned her eyes from Elaine's and, inadvertently, met his. Immediately she was plunged back into the whirlpool of emotions that had battered her earlier, and the next thing she knew, she was smiling and waving from the doorstep and he was turning toward his car.

Elaine watched as his car disappeared down the driveway, then turned to her friend and whooped with excitement. "I did it, Jan! I did it!" She grabbed Janice and whirled her around in an impromptu jig. Flushed and laughing, she sat down on the steps with no regard for the well-tailored pants of her proper business suit.

"Sit down. Wait till you hear this." She patted the step beside her and waited until Janice was settled. "First of all, his company will buy these properties, *both* home and business. Secondly—" she grinned triumphantly at her partner "—we're landscaping the entire development—walkways, parks, even the visitor's center! He was going to do it himself with his own men." She looked over at the dogwoods and azaleas. "It'll mean we can save all these outdoor plants. We can move them immediately, and what's more, start getting paid immediately."

"That means," Janice said, brightening as the implications sank in, "that means we don't have to worry about keeping open throughout the move. We'll have money coming in to tide us over until we're settled again." She clapped her hands together in relief. "I knew you'd do it, Elaine. When I saw that look on your face..."

"What look?" Elaine asked suspiciously, then laughed. "Talk about looks, you should have seen your face when you walked into the shop and saw that beautiful man." She grinned mischievously. "You looked bedazzled, like a schoolgirl in love." She jumped up and pulled Janice to her feet. "Well, now we'll be working at Riverbend Park, and you'll be seeing him all the time." She looked over her shoulder in mock sympathy as she led the way back inside. "Poor man..."

Janice gave her an indignant look, but then, despite herself, she shivered. His touch—she could still feel the electricity that had struck when she'd touched his hand. The very thought of him threatened her. It was one thing to draft a handsome stranger's image into erotic dreams, it was another entirely to be face-to-face with a handsome, independent six-foot-two man whose gaze challenged her in ways she couldn't understand.

So, she'd be seeing him all the time... She shivered again and hurried into the house after Elaine.

Chapter Four

Janice's shoulders sagged as she stood looking into the "studio," so touted by the real estate agent. It was a closet—that was the best that could be said for it. It was too small to turn around in. She shifted weight on her tired feet. In the past week, she'd seen two ranch-style houses, three colonials, a "workman's delight" and a "cottage."

Ranch-style apparently meant one-level, colonial meant anything from small rooms to large pillars, the workman's delight was an uninhabitable mess and the cottage—Janice grimaced as she remembered—the cottage was a converted garage!

She left the real estate agent with mumbled courtesies, her mind reeling from references to "points" and "escrows." This was the kind of situation in which she missed Jay enormously. He had handled all the details of buying their home.

It wouldn't be so bad, she thought, if any of the houses she'd seen so far had been at all attractive. When she thought of leaving her charming old house for one of those things, she shuddered with distaste. It was impossible. She tried to remember what her house had been like before she and Jay had made it a home. Surely it had not been as uninviting as the ones she was now viewing.

Driving home, she wished for an agent who would at least listen to her and make an attempt to find something she could like. As it was, she was hot, tired and disgusted. And her foot on the accelerator felt bruised.

As she turned into her driveway, she felt her spirits lighten. It was so beautiful. The dogwoods were just beginning to turn green, and all around were the glistening new leaves in the sun. She sat in her car for a moment, listening to the birds singing and the wind soughing in the trees.

Just three more weeks. She felt almost despairing as she contemplated the possibilities. If they couldn't find anything, if what they found wasn't immediately available, it it needed work or the paperwork took too long, she and the boys would be forced to move into a motel, or stay with Elaine—who really didn't have the space in her chic Fairfax apartment.

Discouraged, she climbed out of the car and walked slowly around to the kitchen door. It was hot and humid today, a precursor of the Washington area summer. She felt limp and bedraggled, as though wilting from thirst. Her thoughts were muddy, unclear, and the heat had stolen all her enthusiasm.

Elaine was seated at the kitchen table, cool and fresh-looking in a tan cotton safari suit. The air conditioner was running—had obviously been going for some time. Janice immediately felt resentful. She glared at her friend. Elaine never looked tired or upset—she was always immaculate, perfectly tailored and groomed no matter what the situation, and Janice knew she herself looked a mess.

She took a deep breath, felt the sweat cool in rivulets down her back and dropped into a chair. "How do you do it?"

"Do what?" Elaine looked at her blankly. "Good Lord, where have you been? What happened to you? I thought you were going to look at houses."

"I was, and I did. Four houses today, three houses yesterday, and who knows how many tomorrow!" Her exhaustion and discouragement showed in her voice as she propped her elbows on the table and rested her head on her hands. "Elaine...I just don't know." She looked disconsolate. "There's nothing out there that's even worth speaking of. We've been as far as Warrenton—that was the 'cottage.' You've never seen such a sorry sight in your life!"

Elaine shook her head in commiseration and pushed a glass of cold white wine across the table. "Well, you'll find something. There are lots of possibilities for the business, and we can take our time." She watched Janice take a sip from the glass and lean back, the tension draining visibly in the coolness of the house.

Suddenly Janice's eyes opened, and she looked suspiciously at her friend. "Okay, what's going on? What's with the wine, and why are you looking like the cat who swallowed the canary?"

Elaine couldn't hide her grin. She pushed a stack of paper across to Janice. "Here, read."

As Janice began to pull the stack toward her, Elaine burst out, "It's the contract for the landscaping!"

Janice frowned. Sure enough, the paper was covered with legalese.

"Hanrahan just okayed the deal and sent them over. We start work tomorrow!" She grinned. "That Phillips character sure moves fast."

"Tomorrow? But what about a house? Elaine, I just can't spend any time working until I've found a place to move!"

"Oh, honey, I know it's a pain. We'll work something out in time. First, of course, we're going to have to figure out what we want to do there. That's something we can do in the evenings, or whenever you have time. And until the actual planting begins, I can take care of most of the work." She reached across the table to pat her friend's hand. "Come on, cheer up. There's got to be a house around somewhere. You'll find it."

Janice sighed, then, making an effort, lifted the glass and proposed a toast, "Okay, pardner, here's to E & J Garden Center. And to the first big contract we've ever had. And to you."

Elaine smiled, grateful for her attempt at cheer. "And to you, Janice. E & J is on its way up. This time next year—who knows."

By the time Elaine left, Janice was feeling a bit better, but as soon as the door closed behind her, the full frustration of the day came back with a vengeance. Despite Elaine's optimism, one more day had gone by, and she was no nearer to finding a home. What were she and the boys going to do? She hated the thought of having to move someplace temporarily. All her things would have to go into storage. The boys would be dislocated, their activities curtailed. Just when they, as a family, had begun to get over Jay's death, this had to happen. Rather than being able to hold on to the pleasant memories of husband and father, which this house possessed, they had to give it up and start again in a place he'd never touched.

Janice thrust off the feeling of being cast adrift. She would manage, and the boys would settle into any new environment with ease. She shrugged off her feelings of self-pity and washed the glasses in the sink.

Four-thirty. The boys would be home soon. Janice went upstairs to shower and change. Feeling better, or at least fresher, she looked in the refrigerator. "Oh, no. Not leftovers again." She looked in the freezer. It was hopeless. Gyros tonight—Sam's Pizza was getting a lot of their business these days.

At least the boys liked going out—a lot more than she did. Oh, she couldn't wait to have a kitchen she could settle into. She looked around. As the packing progressed, the cozy kitchen she loved had become just another room, losing its familiar charm. In three weeks the wreckers would be coming. She hardened her heart and packed the wineglasses.

The E & J Garden Center van became a fixture at Riverbend Park during the next few days. The two women, Janice in her jeans and flannel shirts, Elaine in her tailored pants and silk blouses, examined, measured and sketched every inch of the development.

So far, construction on the show houses and the public buildings was at the stage of foundation laying. The rest of the property was marked off here and there by little red survey flags. It took a great deal of imagination to visualize the completed development, but David's blueprints and glowing descriptions spurred Janice's creativity. Her drawings of the completed community matched his imaginings so well that he found himself following her around the site whenever she appeared with her sketch pad and crayons.

Janice was happy with the work planning the parks and picnic areas, but the search for a home not only dominated her thoughts, but was beginning to wear her out. Every day she followed up leads given by agents or friends. She even read all the notices on grocery bulletin boards. She'd put at least a thousand miles on her car and had still found absolutely nothing.

* * *

Janice seemed more tired each time David saw her intent upon the plans. The strain of house-hunting, he realized, was definitely beginning to show. She looked pale, her eyes were smudged with weariness, her hair had lost the healthy glow he'd first noticed, and she was beginning to look fragile.

"How's it going?" David asked gently as she tossed her sketch pad and equipment into her car.

Janice gave him a tired smile. "Two more to check out today," she said, pulling off her hat and shaking out her hair. "I don't really expect much anymore, though."

He hated to see her so depressed. "Is there anything I can do to help?"

"Not unless you have the perfect house up your sleeve," she said. Then she seemed to realize her sarcasm. "Oh, I'm sorry." His face had taken on an inward look. "I really didn't mean it that way."

She hesitated, appalled at his withdrawal. She hadn't meant to blame her troubles on him, but his expression was distant as he turned and walked away.

She put out her hand in a hopeless gesture, but he didn't see, and she climbed dispiritedly into her car. So much for miracles and falling in love with a television image, she thought to herself.

David chuckled to himself as she drove off. No, he reminded himself, don't get too excited. It might not work out. He had to call his old friend Charlie right away. If he still wanted to sell Aunt Mabel's old house, it would be perfect for Janice and her sons.

They could even convert that old barn into a shop! Why hadn't he thought of it before?

David phoned Charlie as soon as he got to his trailer.

It was eight o'clock in the morning when Charlie picked up the phone in San Francisco.

"Hey, David. Do you know what time it is? Why d'you think I moved out here in the first place?"

"Couldn't be to get away from your wake-up call, could it?" David laughed.

"Why else? Don't tell me I'm going to have to move to Australia!" Charlie sounded more relaxed than David had heard him sound since the divorce. "As a matter of fact, Dave, I've been offered a partnership in Sydney."

"Sydney! So you're going to join the upside-downers, or is that the out-and-downers?"

"Fu-unny. Want to come along? I've got a foot-locker."

David finally had the chance to ask the question. "Does that mean you're definitely planning to sell the Leesburg house?"

"I hate to. You know how I loved Aunt Mabel and that old place. But I can't go back . . ."

"Well, I might have a buyer for you. Interested?"

"No kidding? Well, the papers are all with my lawyer. Give me a call when you're sure, and I'll send him a power of attorney."

When David put down the phone, he was already visualizing Janice's smile of pleasure. Somehow, over the two weeks he'd known her, that lovely smile and those sparkling eyes had come to— Hold on, he told himself. What are you thinking? The last thing you want is to get involved. Which reminded him that he hadn't called Patricia recently. In fact, his social life, previously active, had dwindled to nothing since the burial ground fiasco. He'd give her a call this evening. But somehow he just couldn't work up much enthusiasm about Patricia as he drove thoughtfully back to the site.

David, in part due to his family, in part to his success in business, was considered a "good catch" in the parlance of Virginia matrons. Ever since high school he'd been courted with increasing intensity by them on behalf of their unmarried daughters. And, of course, most of these daughters were beautiful, wealthy and well-educated. He'd enjoyed the attention; he still did, in fact. He liked women, and they liked him. In this day and age, that was all that was necessary for a relationship, at least on his part. Underlying every one of those willing smiles, he'd detected an almost grim pursuit of status. Imagined or real, it had colored all of his affairs, and he'd never allowed those relationships to go beyond certain bounds.

His life suited him. When he wanted companionship and city lights, they were readily available. When he wanted his privacy and the quiet of a mountain hike with binoculars and a bird book, they were also readily available. He had no one to whom he had to make explanations, or from whom he had to ask permission. And he wanted to keep it that way.

Eventually, of course, he knew that he would like a family—all the things that he'd grown up with. He thought fondly of his parents. They'd been loving and strict, teaching him to have fun while living up to his responsibilities. He pictured himself passing that same attitude along to his own child, and the picture pleased him. But, he thought, not right away.

He picked up the phone to call Janice Haley.

By six o'clock that evening he still hadn't reached her. Somehow the afternoon had dragged. He found himself restless, flitting from one chore to the other, getting more and more frustrated as the day wore on. Now that he'd talked to Charlie, he couldn't wait to show them the house. They'd love it, he gloated, and then they could all concentrate on Riverbend Park.

Still no answer. Frustrated, David locked the trailer and climbed into his Jeep. As he drove onto the highway, he saw Janice's car pull into her driveway, and he followed instinctively.

With a perverse sense of glee, David realized that the house-hunting had been unsuccessful. She looked even more tired than she had earlier.

"Janice," he called.

She looked around with a start. "Oh, hello David." Her surprise turned to welcome as she came over to him.

He'd caught her off guard, and the thrill of seeing him shocked her. Janice still couldn't believe that even after two weeks of working closely with this man, his effect upon her had not diminished in the slightest—if anything, the repeated exposure was heightening her awareness of him.

He looked tense. "Is anything wrong?" she asked as he opened his door.

"No, quite the contrary." His voice had an excited undertone, but his expression was bland.

She glanced at him curiously. This mood, whatever it was, had stripped the businessman from him. Seeing him now, she felt anew that magnetic pull, that attraction. She brought herself up short. What are you thinking? she asked herself in a subdued panic. You barely know him. He's just someone you work with. She hoped none of her confusion showed on her face as she dug out her keys.

"Come on in," she said, leading the way to the kitchen door. "I need a cup of tea. Can I get you anything?" She put down her purse, pulled open the refrigerator and glanced around, wondering vaguely what she had to offer.

"Tea will be fine." He sat down at the kitchen table. "How did it go today?"

She combed her fingers through her hair as she put on the kettle. "The usual," she said dispiritedly. "Nothing even remotely suitable so far. Everything's either too expensive, too run down, or too small. Why do people even bother to build some of these wretched houses, anyway?"

She brought the tea to the table and sat down opposite him. "At least you look cheerful," she said almost resentfully. "What's up?"

David felt cheerful. With a start, he realized that he felt great. "Well, I have a surprise." He stopped and grinned teasingly. "I spoke with my friend Charlie this morning. He's moving to Australia."

"How nice," Janice said perfunctorily.

"Yeah, he's found a new job. He used to live around here." David picked up his cup and sipped. "Umm, nice. What is this?"

"Chamomile." Janice's eyes narrowed. What was he playing at? All of a sudden it all came together—Charlie's house must be for sale. She practically choked on her tea, hiding her smile. Two could play at this game.

"I grow the herbs here. You should try my mint blend sometime. Very nice in the summer. This tea—" she looked innocently at him "—is very good for the digestion. Helps you sleep, too."

He laughed delightedly. The glint in her eye told him she'd figured it out. "Wait till you see it! You're going to love it—it's just perfect."

"Tell me. Tell me about it." Janice leaned forward eagerly.

"Nope. I'll show it to you."

"Let's go."

"Now?" He looked startled, then laughed. "All right. We'd better hurry, though. There's a lot to see."

Janice left a note for Elaine and the boys, grabbed a jacket and hurried after David. A house! And the way he looked—she was so excited that she could barely sit still as he turned the Jeep toward Middleburg.

The country was beautiful. The farther they drove from Centreville, the more rolling the terrain became. And out in front of them, to the west, were the misty, purple outlines of the Appalachians. Route 50 wound through increasingly remote wooded farmland. Just before Middleburg, David turned down the Leesburg road.

"Not far now," he said with a smile. "See there? That's my uncle's horse farm."

"Isn't Oatlands Plantation somewhere near here?" Janice asked.

"Right over there," David said, pointing. He turned off onto a small country road that ran alongside the Oatlands boundary.

"Here?" Janice was ecstatic. "How long has the house been on the market?"

"Since eleven this morning."

She looked at him in amazement. Had he called his friend just for that?

"Charlie's divorce just came through, and he doesn't want to come back here. The house belonged to his great-aunt Mabel. He and I used to run wild on that place, and when she died she left it to him. It's basically in pretty good shape. Charlie camped out there for a while fixing it up, but then he got married, and his wife hated it.

"The marriage only lasted six months, and now he's in California on his way to Australia. So the house has been vacant for almost two years. Charlie and I gave it a good inspection when he inherited it, and it's fundamentally sound."

He stopped the car next to a gravel turnoff. "See that," he said, pointing to a stone hidden among enormous old oak trees. "This is the beginning of the property."

As they drove slowly up the rutted and overgrown driveway, Janice felt as though she were coming home. It was perfect. Even before seeing the house itself, she knew from the surroundings what she would find.

They rounded a last grove of trees, and there it was.

The perfect simplicity of the stone colonial house couldn't be marred by the peeling paint and sagging shutters. Across the top floor, five windows reflected the gloom of overhanging branches. The front door was solid carved oak, mildewed but still sound.

David pulled out his key ring. "Good thing Charlie never asked for his key back." Shaking it, he selected an old-fashioned key and fitted it into the ramshackle lock.

The door creaked open, and Janice and David were assailed by the musty odor of old furniture and torn-up linoleum. Other than the waning evening light they'd let in, the only other light in the hall came filtering through the spiderwebbed transoms at both front and back doors. Janice took a deep breath and coughed. The floors, under a two-year layer of dust and yellowed polyurethane, looked shiny. Janice bent to brush aside the dust. Golden tones of old oak gleamed in the traces left by her fingers.

"Pretty nice, aren't they?" David said, seeing what she'd uncovered. "Charlie and I spent hours sanding and finishing them before he decided not to live here. We didn't get to the upstairs, but with a little work those floors will be just as nice as this one." David led the way through a wood-trimmed arch into a long, rather narrow living room. He crossed the room and pulled threadbare curtains aside. He stepped back quickly, fanning the billows of dust from his face, and sneezed. "Whew!" He opened a French door and stepped carefully onto an old wooden porch.

The long arms of the evening sunlight poured through the opened door. Janice held her breath. The living room was revealed in all its faded elegance. An enormous Adam fireplace was centered in the south wall. Barely visible through the grime, glints of color caught her eye. She scraped away a bit of the dirt. Blue-and-gold patterns on ceramic tiles stared back at her. The entire fireplace was framed in carved wood and inset with these obviously antique tiles of deep blue crackled porcelain with gold highlights.

High ceilings were edged with bas-relief, and a chandelier hung from a center design. The walls were covered with a gloomy pattern of wallpaper, and at its curling edges older colors and patterns showed.

Janice followed David out onto the screened porch. An overgrown flower garden, azaleas, white syringa and a lingering confusion of dogwoods, pressed against the crumbling mesh. In the evening light the lush foliage seemed an enchanted garden. Janice exclaimed in delight, and without thinking she grabbed David's hand and squeezed it. "Oh, David, thank you for bringing me here. It's just perfect." She smiled up at him, her face alight. At the suddenly intent expression in his narrowed eyes, she turned away, dropping his hand in confusion.

What had she done? All of a sudden he was too close, too large—overwhelming. His nearness took her breath away. Her hand still felt the warmth from his, her cheeks burned with her confusion, and she could barely restrain herself from cradling her hand, from reaching up to brush her lips across the memory of that touch.

She jumped as his hand caressed her shoulders. "Janice?" His voice was husky.

She forced herself to look at him, moving away from his hand, a strained smile curving her lips. "Oh, the boys will just love this place."

And she was past him, back in the living room and hurrying toward the hall. David stood foolishly, gazing at her retreating back. What had happened? He could have sworn there, for a moment, that she was ready to come into his arms. And yet, when he'd been ready to oblige, she'd run away. David felt his hunting spirit click into place.

He'd been intrigued by her from the first sight of her slim legs and sexy derriere. He liked her, too. She could be a breath of fresh air in his life, particularly in his love life.

He smiled to himself as he followed her into the hall. As he opened up the library door, he ushered her in with a firm, insistent hand on the small of her back and hid another smile at the shiver that ran through her at the provocativeness of his touch.

Janice sat up late, staring blankly at the test pattern on the television. She could still feel the touch of his hand on her shoulders, on the small of her back.

Was it fear that she felt, or was it something else? There was nothing wrong with having an affair these days—she had no husband she'd be cheating. Jay wouldn't have expected her to spend the rest of her life faithful to a memory.

What was wrong with her? Here she was, with a business to run and a family to raise, and all she could think of was this man who'd suddenly walked into her life.

How had she got herself into this? The magic that had pulled her to him from that first glimpse of his electric eyes haunted her. She couldn't escape her response to him.

And why had David turned out to be so perfect? He was not only good-looking, but kind and sympathetic. An aura of success and security seemed to surround him. Janice didn't kid herself about her need for those qualities in a man. Eight years of marriage to Jay had made that a part of her personality. She'd married before she'd tried to build a life for herself, and she remembered clearly the comfort to be found in being taken care of.

She hugged her pillow tightly. No. It wasn't right, neither for her nor for her children.

And besides, the depth of her feelings for this man had begun to scare her. She would want, no, she would need too much from him. She couldn't fool herself. Everything about him—his boldness, his attempt to kiss her at the house—told her he was looking for an "interlude." She smiled bitterly to herself. She was looking for a lifetime.

Chapter Five

In the clear light of day, the magic of the deserted house and grounds had retreated. The house was just a sadly abandoned house, and the grounds were shamelessly overgrown. There were, however, still enough touches in the tangled garden and the dusty light through the transoms to enthrall Elaine and the children.

"Neat!" Jason and Jonathan plunged into the undergrowth, surfacing at an old sundial. "Wow! What is it?" They leaned forward, examining the old green bronze fittings and scratching lichen from its stone face. Almost instantly, their attention caught by a new marvel, they vanished into the bushes. Their thin, young voices rang clear and bright, pinpointing their location long after they were no longer visible.

Janice, as their voices faded, made as though to follow, a harried frown on her tired face. "I'd better go see what they're up to..."

"You go ahead with Elaine. Show her the house." David took Janice by the arm and guided her gently toward the door. "I'll find those two characters!"

He watched the two women fit the key into the door and disappear into the house. As Janice's excited voice drifted back to him, he smiled. She was a fascinating woman. There were more facets to her than all the women he'd ever known put together. He heard her calling Elaine onto the porch, and the childlike enthusiasm in her voice brought back to him her warmth and strength. She was astonishing. Obviously mature and capable, she was also very sexy to his eyes. Yet, despite her maturity, she didn't seem to realize the effect she had on him. She certainly didn't seem to be making any particular attempt to attract him. She didn't need the careful makeup his other girlfriends seemed to think so essential. She presented herself to the world with all the conflicting facets of her personality. And she didn't expect anything other than that from him. How refreshing that was.

He turned and found the path leading to the pond. The boys' voices seemed to be coming from that direction, and knowing boys, the smell of the water would draw them sooner or later.

He'd forgotten how pleasant this place was. When he was younger, he and Charlie had roamed the old farm, and he still remembered the high points of their exploration. In those days, he thought, batting away a thorny blackberry vine, they'd kept these paths well trampled. It had certainly been easier to play Tarzan then!

He heard the creak of a window being forced open, and Janice's voice drifted out over the jungle. Idly he wondered how long it would take him to break down Janice's defenses. She probably hadn't even gone out with a man since her husband had died. It was going to take patience—that was for sure. He hurried ahead as he heard the boys splashing. Darnit! They'd be wet and muddy—decidedly not the best way to start out trying to win their mother.

Janice struggled with the kitchen window. She and Elaine had made their way through the house, opening windows to let the light in. The boys' voices drifted dimly into the old house. Was it her imagination, or did the house seem to welcome the noise?

"Ugh! Have you looked in the pantry? What did these people eat?" Elaine grimaced. "There's some awfully weird-looking bottled stuff in there." She dusted off her hands and eyed the ceiling. "You've also got a lot of houseguests," she said pointing at the webs clinging thickly in the corners. "I sure don't envy you this cleanup job."

"Oh, it looks worse than it'll be," Janice said distractedly, backing away from one of the walls and eyeing it narrowly. "It's in better condition that I expected under the grime." She grinned at her friend. "You'll love it, Elaine. We'll have some French bread, some cheese and a whole gallon of cold white wine when we're finished." She laughed at the thought of dishpan hands on the delicate stem of a wineglass.

Elaine gave a resigned shake of her head. "I suppose if I don't, you'll never speak to me again."

"That's right," Janice threatened. "Friends help friends move in. Besides, it'll give you something to do while the barn's being rebuilt."

"Have you really made up your mind, then? I think the location is superb for the business. And you can't beat the price. But the house..." She squinted at the peeling wallpaper and uneven flooring. "Are you sure?"

Janice looked at her incredulously. "What do you mean? Of course I'm sure." She looked around the room again. "It's beautiful, just perfect." She pulled Elaine into the dining room. "Just look at that woodwork and the fireplace!"

Elaine tried to see the house through Janice's eyes. The basics were there—that she could see. It was just the amount of work involved. She watched Janice inspect the room. If Janice said it was perfect, then it was. Her friend had a genuine knack for spotting potential, and the tenacity to bring it out. She followed Janice down the hall toward the stairs that twisted to a landing, framing the end of the hall.

"What on earth are you doing?" Elaine questioned as she fanned a thick cloud of dust from her face.

"Look at this!" Janice called excitedly. She tossed a scrap of linoleum aside. "These stairs are made of the same oak as the door." She stood up and peered through the still churning dust. "Here," she said.

With her keys, she scratched at the doorframe that led into the study. "I'll bet it's all oak. And look at that carving..." She brushed the cobwebs away from the newel post, revealing the intricately carved head of a cat. "I've never seen anything like that. I wonder who did it... and why." She made herself a note to ask David.

"Well, let's have a look." She grasped the banister and tested it, then, an eager look on her face, she slowly, gingerly, mounted the stairs.

Elaine watched, horrified, as Janice recklessly ran up to the landing.

"Look, there are the boys." Janice turned around to find Elaine. Her friend was still motionless in the hall, her expression clearly revealing her distrust of the stairs. Janice laughed. "Come on, they're perfectly safe." She stamped her foot, and dust billowed around her slender form. Impatiently she turned and tried the window. With a groan of protest, the counterweights in the frame moved a few inches, then stuck tight. "Drat!" She cleared a small spot with her fingertips and peered through the grimy window.

Elaine heard a thin, faint hail and carefully, testing each step, made her way to Janice's side.

"Hi," Janice called to the boys, waving and smiling.

The boys and David waved back, then continued up the narrow streambed. David was loaded down with three pairs of shoes. He had rolled up his jeans to just below his knees. His calves were tanned and strongly muscled, probably from riding, Janice thought as she watched him move with lithe grace through the silver-and-green dancing waters. The turn of his head, the wide shifting of his shoulders and back as he bent toward her sons . . .

Janice couldn't bring herself to draw away from the wild magic she saw in him that afternoon. She had to will herself to keep from reaching for him. Every movement compelled her whole being, singing a powerful and sensuous song through her veins, until the light dazzled her eyes and his form faded into the shadows. She blinked.

"Oh, look," Elaine said, grabbing Janice's arm and pointing while she laughed.

The seat of David's jeans showed unmistakable evidence of a spill.

She joined Elaine's laughter. Then, arm in arm, the two women braved the remainder of the stairs to explore the second level.

Jason poked at a moss-covered rock, half submerged in the shallow water. Jonathan was busy ambushing water bugs. Whenever the ambush was successful, he shrieked with glee and brought his catch to David for admiration. David's pockets were already heavy with interesting rocks they'd found along the way. He grinned to himself. If these boys were anything like him, the great discoveries would soon be replaced by other marvels.

As the two boys foraged ahead, he found himself observing them with surprised pleasure. Boys never changed, no matter what happened to the world around. He remembered clearly scampering around barefoot, collecting rocks and splashing after the

long-legged skittering bugs that inhabited all the favorite haunts of youth. He'd forgotten what it was
like to be a child—or perhaps it took the presence of
that youthful joy in discovery to bring back those
memories. He realized that his life didn't include
children. None of the friends and family he saw had
children; the closest he came was seeing them walk
to school as he drove by.

There was something extra, though, that he liked
about watching Jason and Jonathan. Like a faint
echo, he caught intimations of their mother. It wasn't
so much in their looks, which must have come from
their father, but in their intent involvement with
whatever they happened to be doing. Sometimes, a
fleeting expression brought Janice vividly to mind.

He liked these boys.

He glanced up at the window where she'd been
standing. He liked her, too.

The air was slightly hazy, the distant mountains
almost invisible. It was almost noon, hot and still,
and bees headed mindlessly in direct lines from one
wildflower to another along the drive. Janice and
Elaine kept to the shade as they walked slowly
through the heat to the ruins of the barn near the
property line.

Janice pulled the hair away from her neck and
fanned herself with a dusty hand. Although it was
still only May, the fickle Washington area weather
was playing its yearly tricks. The previous evening
had been chill enough to call for building a fire, and
yet today the sun blazed with all the strength of

midsummer. Janice wished she'd brought a thermos full of ice water.

Just ahead, Elaine came to a halt. "Here it is." As Janice came up beside her, she was grimly surveying the remains. One almost complete stone wall towered solitary under a curtain of vines. The other three walls appeared only as overgrown mounds of stone and broken wood.

The two women stood in silence. It was much worse than they'd expected. The roof had fallen in some years before and was now a mangled mess of rusty metal sheets.

"Well, at least we won't have to call in a lumber company to clear out the floor space. These trees can't be more than four or five years old." She tested the balance of a pile of tumbled stones, then gingerly climbed to a better vantage point.

Janice was unreasonably disappointed. She picked up a piece of wood and flung it into the undergrowth. "It's a total loss," she said disgustedly. "We'll have to clear the whole area and buy a prefab."

"Oh, no, you don't," David's voice came emphatically from behind her. "That whole wall back there is solid enough." He scrambled over the mess to stand in the old barn enclosure, followed by two flagging but still energetic boys. "Parts of these other three walls can be salvaged, too. We'll use some of the stone for the rebuilding, and the rest can be used as paving both inside and out. The only part that will have to be entirely rebuilt will be the roof, and that means you can have any kind of skylights or window vents you like."

"Yes, great," Elaine said sarcastically. "And how long is all that going to take?"

"A lot less time than you think," David said, his enthusiasm soaring as he looked around and pictured the finished product. Seeing Elaine's continued frown, he grinned at her mockingly. "What'd you expect? To buy a place for five thousand dollars and just walk right in?" He saw Janice start to pick her way delicately over the rubble and went to help her, appreciating the smooth, firm curves of her hips and thighs and the gentle pressure of her breasts against her Indian cotton blouse as she threw out her arms for balance. His strong hands closed about her waist. Grinning wickedly into her surprised eyes, he swung her around and slowly lowered her to the ground, his body brushing lightly against hers, searing her, branding her with the promise of ecstasy.

Janice could barely keep herself from pressing closer, from automatically responding, but the boys were there, and Elaine's speculative eyes were on her. She pushed herself almost frantically away from the provocative touch of his body, but as she turned to pass him, he put his arm around her shoulders and squeezed her slightly. "You'll see, it'll be great by the time it's finished."

But her knees felt weak, her heart pounded, and her breath came short. His touch, so casually friendly yet so intimate, made her feel weak. And she could feel, despite his easy tone, that he was as tense as she. His arm trembled against her shoulders.

All day after that moment in the ruined barn, Janice could sense David, no matter where he was. Her nerve ends seemed sensitive to his very presence, as though an electric current had been established between them, throwing sparks that Janice marveled no one else could see.

The next few days both sped and dragged. Janice was constantly aware of David and almost as constantly in his company. Charlie's lawyer drew up all the papers with record speed, but both of them had to be present at every meeting. Each time David touched her, the world seemed to stop. But between these meetings time slowed to a crawl, and Janice packed, cleaned and waited.

When the papers on the house were finally complete, Janice and David were called to the lawyer's office. The lawyer was delighted. It had been the easiest and quickest sale he'd ever been involved with.

Twenty minutes later, after handshakes all around, she and David left the lawyer's office. Clutching the folder containing her title to Little Creek Farm, Janice couldn't keep a triumphant grin from her face, and David, glancing at her, shook his head in wonder at the transparent delight that transformed her.

They stood on the sidewalk in front of the Leesburg lawyer's office. It was just after five o'clock—time enough for her to run out there to gloat, Janice thought. For the first time in her entire life, she'd made the decision, she'd signed the papers, and it was her money that had bought the house. She could hardly wait to stand on her own property. She took a deep breath of the evening air and turned to David. "I feel just wonderful."

Her enthusiasm was contagious. His own spirits rose, and he took her by the shoulders, leaned down to that glowing face and gave her a big kiss on the forehead. "Come on, honey," he said impulsively, "let's celebrate. How about dinner?"

He saw her response before she answered. Her face showed a flattering mixture of desire and regret. "I'd love to, David, but I just can't wait to get out there and admire my house."

His face softened as he looked down at her. "I'll tell you what," he said impulsively. "I'll pick up some champagne and meet you out there. How's that?"

She nodded, too excited to speak. For a moment they stood facing each other, neither one apparently wanting to make the first parting move. Then Janice turned and almost ran to her car.

As she drove off, her feelings were so confused that she felt twisted into knots. What had she done? All the reasons she'd reviewed with herself as to why she shouldn't get involved with David were still valid. She was falling in love with him—more so now that she knew him better. And she was still too vulnerable and could easily be hurt by him if he wasn't willing to take a chance on a lifetime commitment.

Janice clenched her hands on the wheel. What would she do? What could she do? Maybe she was reading too much into his attentions. The relief that this thought should have brought her was submerged by the hollow feeling of fear. Was she wrong?

No! She couldn't be that wrong. She had felt the tension in him when she was near. She'd seen the way he'd looked at her. She was as sure as she could be that he desired her.

Throughout the rest of the drive Janice found herself going over and over these same thoughts. As she pulled up to the house, she found herself in a frenzy of indecision. She could barely see the house in the twilight. After a long moment, she left the car and wandered around back. She sat on the porch, and looked blankly into the tangled garden.

The Jeep's engine growled softly up the drive. David peered through the windshield. There was her car. The house loomed dark and depressingly empty, and David felt his heart sink. Somehow he'd expected candlelight and soft music—all the trappings of his usual romances.

He turned off the engine and sat listening to the gentle sounds of the countryside. Gradually the evening's peace seeped into him. The beautiful, varied warble of a mockingbird's dusk-time song floated through the tangled limbs of the neglected garden, and David slowly stood to listen. Under the trees, the shadows grew deeper as the sun sank lower in the sky, and here and there tiny flares of light marked the wandering paths of fireflies. David's disappointment vanished in an instant. What could be more romantic than the serenade of a wild bird in the night and the gentle sparkle of fireflies drifting through the woods?

He picked up the basket and the chilled bottles and quietly, so as not to disturb the gray songster, made his way around the house. Somehow he'd known he would find her on the back porch. It overlooked the old sundial, which was surrounded by a tangled profusion of ivy and overgrown wild roses.

She was sitting on the steps of the porch, leaning back against the solid wooden railing. She looked so fragile—so beautiful. The proper white business suit she'd worn to the lawyer's office was softened by her posture and, in the twilight, adorned her as if it were silk and lace.

Desire took hold of him and his steps quickened. He knelt on the steps beside her, holding his breath as she slowly turned to him. Reluctance and suppressed passion visibly warred across her countenance. David put aside the champagne and the picnic. He took her hand in his, noting with renewed excitement how it trembled in his clasp, and drew her with him into the softly scented grass of their own magic garden.

Janice felt as though she couldn't breathe. His lips brushed the tips of her fingers, and she felt the thrill of that touch race through her entire being. His lips moved slowly across her palm, along her arm, her shoulder, seeming to leave a trail of fire in their wake that overwhelmed her senses and sent shock waves through her, igniting a core of passion that she had never dreamed existed. Her hand reached, her fingers caressed, her mouth demanded his—and, as the moon rose above the magic garden, her lips yielded to his with joy.

One long, breathless kiss, another, and then they broke apart. Janice was drained as she pulled away, passion and desire had warred with her better judgment. David could barely stand the tension between them, but she looked so trusting, so vulnerable, that he could not bring himself to take advantage of the situation. Instead, with an effort greater than any other he could remember making, he turned away, breaking the magical contact of their eyes, and reached for the picnic basket...

The moon set as they sat beneath the waxing light of the stars, carefully not touching. Her eyes followed the outline of his shoulders, his profile, while her hand ceaselessly caressed the stem of the champagne flutes, fingers trembling with the effort of keeping from him.

From the inky blackness under the trees lining the barely audible stream, came the haunting call of a night-hunting owl. Janice shivered. The sound seemed to pierce her, warning her. Beside her, David shifted restlessly. He whispered, "Barn owl," as the call came again.

In companionable silence they listened to the cicadas and night birds, until David opened up the picnic basket and reached inside.

Elaine's car was still in the lot when Janice got home, but the house was in complete darkness. The boys! She'd forgotten all about them. She sat weakly in the car, hoping Elaine wasn't too angry at being kept so late. Embarrassment engulfed her as she remembered how easily she had abandoned all thought at the first touch of his lips. Even the memory of him now made desire for his touch well up in her. She looked at the darkened windows, and suddenly she was crying helplessly, the tears rolling unhindered down her cheeks. What had she done?

Janice tiptoed through the kitchen, upstairs, and checked the boys' room. They were sleeping, peacefully, unaware that their mother had forgotten their very existence. She looked into the guest room. Elaine's clothes were neatly folded on the dresser, and the sounds of her even breathing reached Janice in the hall. She continued to her own room, closing the door behind her as though to protect that peaceful existence from the tumultuous passions that she could barely control. The very air she breathed felt different—more alive somehow, dangerously unpredictable.

How could she have done it?

Her fingers brushed her lips, remembering the magic of his touch. She recoiled and caught a glimpse of herself in the old cheval mirror. Her cheeks were flushed, and her eyes glistened. She moved closer, fascinated by the changes this one night had wrought. She no longer recognized herself. Close up, she saw the lines around her eyes, the gray in her hair stealing her youth strand by silver strand. She was no longer as slim, as taut as she had been, fatigue darkened her eyes with shadowy smudges and her skin looked sallow in the yellow light of her bedside lamp.

What must he have thought of her?

She blushed, wishing for time to turn back. If only she were younger, or he older. She threw herself on the bed and hugged the pillow to herself. She imagined herself—younger, slim, beautiful, free...

No! She sat up abruptly.

She loved her boys—loved them with all her heart. How could she wish for anything to be different? If it were, she would not have them, and that thought was unbearable.

Chapter Six

Janice sat up in bed, rubbing her tired eyes. It was another morning—the third since her picnic with David in the moonlight.

The rose-tinted light of dawn filtered across the quilt, picking out the faded green of trailing patch-work leaves. She felt as though she hadn't slept at all since that evening at her new house with David.

He would surely call today.

She found herself recalling everything—the touch of his hands, the thrill of his lips on hers, even the memory of his embrace under the moonlight, with the fresh green smell of the surrounding woods and the small rushing whisper of the tiny creek in the background. Janice shivered and huddled closer into the covers. Her senses reeled, and she struggled for control.

How many times had she told herself that it was folly to get involved with David? She was losing control. Until the moment she had allowed him to touch her, she'd been safe—lonely but safe. Now she feared the future, feared the day he would turn to someone else. Janice buried her face in her hands.

The first of the day's string of construction vehicles rumbled by, penetrating even here, in the quiet fastness of her safe retreat.

David. She felt again the shock of desire that had struck her when she'd first seen him, the electric vision that had changed her forever by opening her eyes to the poverty of her emotional life. She remembered the magic of his eyes meeting hers and the first handshake that had brought the vision to life. Janice's eyes opened in panic. She gasped for breath and swung her legs from the embracing warmth of the tangled covers.

She couldn't afford to desire him, knowing that she'd be hurt, but she couldn't keep from loving him, whatever the price. It was too late to stop, to retreat. Perhaps it had been too late from the moment she'd caught that fateful newscast. She felt both free and wildly out of control, as though carried along in a tumultuous rush of wind. There was fear, yes, but there was also an exultation that shivered through her veins and called relentlessly to her lonely heart.

The alarm rang, a mundane sound in the midst of her passions. Janice reluctantly rose, splashed water on her sheet-creased cheeks and pulled on the caftan Randy had sent her last year from Egypt. She ran her hands over the cotton embroidery. David would like this, she thought, looking anxiously into the mirror. She quickly brushed some life into her tangled hair, vigorously yanking at the snarls and smoothing the static from it. She frowned into the mirror. Still too pale. Hurriedly she rubbed a dab of rouge over her cheekbones. Her eyes were large and shadowed, but she didn't have time to do anything else. Next door she could hear the first faint sounds of Jason's waking.

A wave of tenderness came over her as she dropped the rouge into the sink and quietly went down to the kitchen. In a burst of energy, she whipped up pancakes, feeling more alive by the minute, and was able to greet her sons cheerfully when they came jostling in for breakfast.

Fifteen minutes later, the pancakes and the boys both gone, she hummed as she stacked the dishwasher and poured more coffee. Now I'll do some packing, she thought as she looked at the flattened boxes standing against the living room wall.

She put on another pot of coffee, knowing that if David came by he would surely want some, and then started folding down the flaps of cardboard to make a box. It was eight o'clock. She hurried, hoping to have something accomplished for the morning.

Half an hour later, the empty cartons in the corner of the room mocked Janice as she stared despairingly at them from the kitchen doorway.

Three whole days, she thought miserably. Why hadn't he called back? The agonized waiting was unbearable, but she refused to chase after him.

At times she was almost glad he hadn't come around the next morning. Her life, all the plans she'd made, none of them had room for him, and the pain of not hearing from him was almost balanced by the relief of knowing herself free to continue on the path she'd chosen and worked for.

But that was only at times. Lurking around every corner of her day was the longing his arms and lips had awakened.

The day after that magical evening with David she'd found a garbled message in Elaine's handwriting on the back of an old envelope, telling her that she'd received a phone call. And then, later that same evening, she'd got out of her car and run up the walk when she heard the lonely clamor of the telephone ringing inside her house. She'd fumbled with purse, keys and doorknob, but when she reached for the phone and picked it up, all she'd heard was a click and the empty sound of the dial tone. It had to have been David.

Isolated in time, that night was a separate instant, dividing her life into before and after. Before, Janice had been Jay's wife, stable, established. Now, after that kiss, she was something unfinished, waiting to be completed. All her hard-won independence didn't keep her from watching the clock, counting the minutes.

Each moment of each hour of each day that passed without word from him buried her deeper in limbo. She was able to do what was necessary. The work crews had been scheduled to clear up the debris at the nursery's new site, and a cleaning service was giving the house a thorough work over before the painters arrived. Electricians, plumbers and a roofing inspector were lined up for next week, and packed boxes were piling up in every available space, waiting for the go-ahead on the move.

All of these things she could do; she was used to ordering supplies and overseeing workmen. But, against her will, her heart waited, waited in increasing panic for David to call.

Janice returned to the living room again and ran down her mental list of preparations. The major furniture wasn't going to be any problem. She'd long ago learned to leave it to the professionals. What always amazed her was the sheer volume of odds and ends that even a relatively empty, tidy room managed to hold. She'd already filled one box with magazines and books, yet the room looked untouched.

Somehow her earlier enthusiasm had drained away, just as the lovely dawn had faded into a lackluster morning, taking her small burst of energy with it.

She turned back to the kitchen. With a fresh cup of coffee replacing the full cold cup she'd just tossed out, she eased herself onto a wooden chair and propped her chin on her hands. She closed her eyes. Where was he? Elaine said he hadn't been at the site for more than an hour and a half at a time. Had she totally misread him that night? Had she been a fool? No! Janice couldn't believe that David, knowing he'd eventually have to face her at work, could have been so callous. His nature wasn't callous, not unless she'd totally lost all her senses!

She glanced at the clock. A quarter to nine. She couldn't just sit there any longer, but neither could she stand the thought of driving to Riverbend Park and possibly seeing him. What had happened? Had she been too eager? Had she driven him away? What had she done? The few times she'd gone to the site to clarify her landscape blueprints, he hadn't been around. Most of her work now had to be done in her own office, and that, plus the work of preparing for the move, had kept her away.

And how, she asked herself as she climbed the stairs again, how was it possible to ache in all the places she ached? If only she could wake up. Her eyes felt heavy as she turned on the shower and tested the water's warmth. The mirror this morning hadn't been kind. It showed the sleepless rings under her eyes, the paleness that made her feel even more tired than she actually was.

Now, blessedly, the heat began to fog up the bathroom, and in a few moments she couldn't see the mirror anymore. The warm water eased her aching muscles and relaxed her, so that when she wrapped herself in the towel and came back into her bedroom, she couldn't resist curling up under the covers for just five more minutes.

When she opened her eyes again, it was ten o'clock. She felt better, more alive. Janice climbed into her working clothes and approached the mirror again. Oh, definitely, she thought. Much, much better. She sipped the coffee Elaine had left on her bedside table and pulled on a clean pair of socks.

David... Janice blinked back the tears as she thought of him. How could such a short time make such a drastic difference? No matter what happened with David, in less than one month, her life had been enriched in ways she never could have expected. Even if missing that one phone call meant she'd never see him again, she always had the memory of that one night. At this thought, the full remembrance of how she'd spent that night came back. Janice stared at the wall as she remembered the satin darkness, the touch of her lover's heated skin and her own seesawing emotions.

Suddenly it all seem so unreal. She could no longer recognize in herself the person of any of those memories. She shook her head. The extra half hour of sleep seemed to have cleared her mind admirably, and she began to feel ready to deal with her life and all of its complications again—even David.

"Janice," Elaine called from the stairs. "I see you got some packing done this morning," she snickered.

"Sure," Janice yelled back. "As much as you did yesterday!"

The two friends grinned at each other from opposite ends of the stairwell.

"Hurry down! I've just put on some fresh coffee, and there's something you have to see."

"Be right there," Janice called to Elaine's back. She brushed her hair, feeling more cheerful than she had for days, and hurried downstairs.

David's elbows were sprawled all over the kitchen table, which was strewn with large sheets of paper covered with fine lines and measurements. His eyes were shadowed, but his countenance was relaxed, at peace. He met her eyes squarely, and she glowered at him. How dare he wander into her house like that after three days of silence! Janice was uncomfortably aware that her heart was suddenly racing, and her cheeks glowing with excitement, which only made her angrier. After all this time, just when she'd begun to regain her equilibrium, he waltzed into her kitchen with his Riverbend Park plans, expecting what—a welcome? Open arms?

He seemed, if anything, intrigued by her anger, and winked shamelessly at her when Elaine was at the counter filling the mugs.

Janice was so angry she couldn't speak!

"And to think—if we like it, we could have Harvey begin as soon as the ground is cleared," Elaine said as she turned back to the table, balancing three mugs carefully. "Clear a spot, there, Janice. Let's see what David's got. He refused to show me without you."

Janice knew how sharp Elaine could be. She struggled to control her temper and noncommittally cleared a corner for the tray, hoping her friend would not pick up on the byplay between David and herself. With an effort, she forced herself to relax and sip the coffee as David sorted the sheets of paper and began to present his ideas for the new garden center building.

Elaine was rapt, absorbed in the talk of west and south light, elevations, built-in shelving, heating and vents and double storm doors to save energy. Janice watched David's hand trace the delicate pen lines around the paper, but her mind kept wandering to his touch, the delicate control of his fingertips. With a snap, she looked up to find his eyes on hers with an expression in them that she recognized and had begun to fear. She felt hunted and could barely keep herself from leaving, running from the challenge and promise in those dark eyes.

"How about this, Janice?" Elaine demanded. "Doesn't this seem a bit large for us? We'd have to hire someone to help keep an eye on it all."

Janice blinked herself into focus.

"No, you wouldn't," David interrupted. "The beauty of this type of building is that you can screen off areas as securely as you like, without losing the overall feeling of openness."

While Janice listened to David's enthusiasm for his project, vaguely understanding what he was saying, a part of her was being inexorably drawn into the game of seduction he seemed to be playing with her. A shudder, whether of fear or pleasure, ran through her each time she became aware of his intent gaze. She felt as though the stakes had been raised, that what was happening now would have long-range implications. David was weaving himself into her life in such a way that would necessitate close contact for an extended length of time. The building, his involvement as architect, and even his sparring relationship with Elaine, all argued for his continued presence in their lives.

The shop bell rang. Elaine looked over at Janice's bemused expression, then hurried to answer its sum-

SILHOUETTE DELIVERS FIRST-CLASS ROMANCE— DIRECT TO YOUR DOOR

Mail the Heart sticker on the postpaid order card today and you'll receive:

— **4 new Silhouette Romance novels—FREE**
— **an elegant pen & watch set—FREE**
— **and a surprise mystery bonus—FREE**

But that's not all. You'll also get:

Free Home Delivery

When you subscribe to Silhouette Romance, the excitement, romance and faraway adventures of these novels can be yours for previewing in the convenience of your own home. Every month we'll deliver 6 new books right to your door. If you decide to keep them, they'll be yours for only $1.95 each. And there is no extra charge for shipping and handling!

Free Monthly Newsletter

It's the indispensable insider's look at our most popular writers and their upcoming novels. Now you can have a behind-the-scenes look at the fascinating world of Silhouette! It's an added bonus you'll look forward to every month!

Special Extras—FREE

Because our home subscribers are our most valued readers, we'll be sending you additional free gifts from time to time as a token of our appreciation.

OPEN YOUR MAILBOX TO A WORLD OF LOVE AND ROMANCE EACH MONTH. JUST COMPLETE, DETACH AND MAIL YOUR FREE OFFER CARD TODAY!

Remember! To receive your free books, pen and watch set and mystery gift, return the postpaid card below. But don't delay!

DETACH AND MAIL CARD TODAY.

MAIL THE POSTPAID CARD TODAY!

BUSINESS REPLY MAIL

FIRST CLASS PERMIT NO. 194 CLIFTON, N.J.

Postage will be paid by addressee

**Silhouette Books
120 Brighton Road
P.O. Box 5084
Clifton, NJ 07015-9956**

NO POSTAGE
NECESSARY
IF MAILED
IN THE
UNITED STATES

mons. Her voice, echoing in the wide open house, began to explain that the shop was now closed. As Janice stood to clear the table, she heard Elaine walk to the desk to get the customer one of their "moving" cards.

David's arms came around her from behind. His warm breath stirred the fine tendrils of hair on her neck as he hugged her to him. The whole length of his body pressed against hers, and she closed her eyes and relaxed into his embrace. All the confusion of the past few days seemed to drain from her in his arms. She felt renewed, stronger, as if he were lending his strength to her.

His lips brushed against her ear, sending chills of excitement through her nerve endings. He whispered, "Mmm, you feel so good," his voice, low and husky with emotion. He rocked her gently in his arms, his lips trailing kisses of fire across her throat, his hands seeking the soft roundness of her breasts. "Tonight?" Urgently he turned her toward him, searching her eyes for an answer. "I have to see you..."

Helplessly Janice wanted to nod, all her defenses overcome by the rush of memories his embrace awoke in her of the night in the moonlit garden. "Ten o'clock?" he asked. His whisper was warm, intimate, his breath a gentle caress against her ear. She felt herself weakening, all her senses crying out for the ecstasy of his touch, of his lips on hers.

Frantically Janice wrenched free of his embrace. Three days without a word, and now he expected to waltz in at ten o'clock at night? No! She had to be strong. This untamed desire could destroy her and all she held dear. Unwilling to meet his eyes, knowing that his gaze could undo her fragile resolve, she braced herself against the counter and stared out the kitchen window. Shaking off the hand he placed on her shoulder, she took a steadying breath and turned to face him. For a moment she couldn't speak. She didn't recognize this man. His intent desire, any tenderness he'd shown, had now disappeared. If he felt anything, it was hidden behind a cynical exterior—as though a mask had come down, shielding whatever emotion he truly felt.

For the first time, Janice saw the formidable stranger who was part of the David Phillips she was coming to know. This was the aspect of the man who had made his business a success so quickly, who dealt with the world of finances and contracts as she never could.

Feeling as though she were betraying every hope in her life, Janice spoke to the stranger in a voice she barely recognized. "No. Don't come. I can't play these games with you. I have my life and my children." Janice blinked away angry tears. "I won't deny that I want you. I can't deny it. But, I still have the strength to turn my back on you. I refuse to sacrifice everything that's important to me, even for you."

David's mask slipped for a moment. He looked shocked, as though she'd hit him. Then his features rearranged themselves again, and thankfully Janice saw this distant David standing before her smile tightly as Elaine came back into the room.

He took his leave politely, leaving the plans for the nursery on the kitchen table. Janice didn't see him to the door but could almost feel his presence withdrawing, leaving the house, the property and maybe her life.

Unable to feel anything, she moved through the evening and the next day in a frozen well of silence. She felt detached from herself, going through the motions of packing, cooking and mothering without truly being involved.

Once or twice she attempted to break through the icy detachment that preserved her in this unnatural calm, but each time she was aware of a storm of emotion that lay in wait for her, and could only draw back again. David—how long had it been? Would she ever see him again?

She marveled in a detached way at how slowly time passed. Only twelve hours, she thought as she taped another box...only twenty-four hours as she drove past the cleanup crew clearing the rubble from the old barn...thirty-six hours as she, dry-eyed and dusty, turned on the news but couldn't watch it...seventy-five hours, she thought in surprise as she unloaded the first of the cartons in the new house. The cleaners had done a passable job, and she stacked the boxes in the corner as the movers came up the path behind her.

Elaine stood on the landing, directing the traffic upstairs while Janice supervised the unloading of the furniture for the ground floor. By the time Elaine left to pick up the boys, the new house, apart from packing materials in piles and leftover boxes, was almost like home. All the furniture had been found comfortable niches, and the small pictures and boxes of books for the living room had been unpacked and mostly put into place. Upstairs the beds were made, and the drawers had been put back in the dressers. The rest of the house was a shambles. The larger furniture was placed approximately where it was to go, but boxes lined the walls and rose in heaps to the ceiling.

Janice sank wearily onto the lowest stair and surveyed the chaos. She shrugged, unable to muster any strong emotion, and slowly climbed to her feet and wandered through the now-quiet rooms. The electricity had been turned on the day before, and she plugged in lamps as she passed, leaving a golden wake of light behind her.

The slam of a car door was followed by running footsteps and excited young voices. "Mom. Mom, look what we've got!" Jason and Jonathan pounded into the kitchen and deposited two large pizza boxes on the counter.

Janice smiled. "What a good idea. Did you get extra cheese and sausage on one?" Jason nodded. "And mushrooms and olives on the other," he said importantly.

Janice grinned. "Here," she said, ruffling his hair as she grabbed a tablecloth from an open box. "Go spread this out on the porch. We'll have a picnic."

"Elaine's getting drinks and ice," Jason called as the boys raced from the kitchen.

"No running." Janice dug into the box with paper plates and napkins, then straightened. She hadn't heard the car drive off again. Where was Elaine?

She turned with the plates in her hand, and there stood David. For a moment she couldn't move. The cold, alien look she'd encountered when she'd last seen him had disappeared, leaving no trace. He smiled challengingly, and Janice felt the ice break as the tension dissipated. A grin spread across his face as she smiled shakily at him, the paper plates slipping to the floor like falling leaves.

In one flowing movement, David picked up the paper plates, grabbed napkins and gently pushed her through the kitchen door. "Hurry up," he said in a voice that was unexpectedly tender. "Elaine should be here in a moment, and we're all starving."

The remainder of the evening passed in a haze for Janice. They all sat cross-legged on a myriad of assorted cushions dragged haphazardly from boxes. The adults sampled a local vintage wine—all Elaine had been able to find at the nearest store—and Jason and Jonathan happily downed their colas. The wine was surprisingly good, and David regaled the two women with stories of the numerous local vineyards and wine festivals in and around Middleburg.

Janice laughed until her sides hurt at some of his anecdotes. David's ready charm and natural humor filled the house, and Janice was glad that her family's first night in their new home was made memorable by such a warm, relaxed gathering. The boys, as the hour grew late, became rowdy due to the unaccustomed excitement of the day, and Janice finally had to chase them upstairs to their new bedrooms, where the final excitement was to weave their way to their beds through the piles of boxes still taped shut.

Jonathan, only six years old and very tired but unwilling to let go of the party, began to cry. Tears of frustrated exhaustion glimmered on his cheeks as Janice tried unsuccessfully to settle him. The moment she turned to cajole Jason, Jonathan was squirming out of the covers and trying to slip past her.

"Who wants a story?"

Janice brushed the hair from her eyes and looked gratefully at David, who was standing in the doorway. Jonathan was out of bed again, tugging at David's hand and looking appealingly over his shoulder at his mother. "Story, story!" he cried as his little hands drew David over to his bedside.

Janice caught David's eye, and at her questioning look he smiled reassuringly. "Go on downstairs. Elaine's making coffee. I'll be down in a moment."

As she slowly headed downstairs, her trailing hand slipping lovingly over the time-polished wood of the banister, she heard his deep voice melodiously drawing out the story of a boy and his beautiful black horse.

Janice leaned back against the heaped-up cushions on the porch and pulled her jacket tight. She felt a languorous contentment. The small sounds of Elaine making coffee, of David's voice rumbling from above, the creaks and whispers of the trees beyond the screen, combined to form a lullaby that soothed her raw nerves of the past few days. She felt absurdly happy, as though everything would some-how work out. She snuggled closer into the cush-ions, happier than she could remember being for years. She smiled to herself, and the moonlight frac-tured through the screen, wavering over the hard-wood floor.

Elaine walked softly, carefully balancing the tray of coffee and cups. As she stopped to place it on the floor, she glanced at Janice, froze, then stood up, taking the tray with her back into the kitchen.

"David." Elaine's whisper caught him as he headed for the porch. He looked across the room. Elaine's contorted face elaborately mouthed, "She's asleep," from the dimness of the hall. David invol-untarily looked toward the porch, his heart sud-denly racing at the thought of Janice curled up there among the cushions, but Elaine's whisper caught at him before he took a step. He turned, wrenching himself away from that vision. They stood compan-ionably in the kitchen, leaning against the counter, drinking coffee from cups Elaine had dug out of a small box, and discussed all the chores still to be done before Monday.

During the coming week, beginning early Mon-day morning, all the trees and shrubs from the old garden center would have to be moved, or be lost to the bulldozers. Both Janice and Elaine were going to have long, hard hours of work ahead of them. This weekend would be the only time available for Jan-ice's family to unpack and get comfortably settled.

Elaine planned to help both Saturday and Sunday, or until the house was livable.

Elaine let several broad hints drop about the things that needed doing, such as putting up bookshelves, moving furniture and chopping wood. David, amused, allowed himself to be persuaded into promising his time. She looked so pleased with herself for having cornered him that he mercifully kept his mouth shut about his own intentions; invitation or not, nothing could have kept him away.

He'd been furious when Janice had thrown him out. But over the next few days that fury had died down, and he'd been able to think. Love—David wasn't even sure what the word meant. He did know that not one of the women he'd known in the past and had thought that he loved had inspired him as this one, rather quiet woman did. From his first glimpse of her, her wren-brown hair and large, shadowed eyes had drawn him. Both the shock of being pushed away and the intensely painful emotion he'd glimpsed in her as she had done so had shaken him, and he'd realized that he couldn't let go. Janice was someone new, different, and his whole being cried out to get to know and understand her.

Their embraces beneath the summer moon now seemed like a dream—a vision of what love could be, or a promise for the future. David had already made up his mind: he had to chase the dream to know if it was the promise he imagined it could be.

Once the decision had been made, he'd worked out his strategy. It was fortunate that Janice had to move, for she couldn't easily refuse help. Another piece of good fortune was the coming week of transporting and transplanting. David and Janice would naturally come together often while the work was in progress at Riverbend. Lastly—and David knew that this could be the telling factor—he genuinely liked Jason and Jonathan. What might have seemed a cold-blooded use of their affections was in truth a pleasure that he didn't want to deny himself. It had literally been years since he'd had anything to do with children, and Janice's sons were a continual delight in their unfeigned enjoyment of his company. He'd already planned to take them riding. He even caught himself thinking how much they would like his favorite trails.

David had no doubts about his ability to have an affair with Janice—he'd seduced enough willing women to be sure of that. He was, however, still haunted by the feeling that there were untapped depths to a relationship with her that would prove more promising, more rewarding than anything he'd previously experienced. It was this feeling that had made him restrain himself with her the other night. He was afraid that if he made the wrong move he would lose Janice altogether and never find out what riches might lie in the future.

While Elaine threw out the crumpled napkins and plates and rinsed the cups, David wandered onto the porch and stood pensively, looking down at the curled figure of the woman who'd so bemused him. Janice wore a smile, and the moonlight cast her and the porch into a black-and-white painting that would forever remain in his memory. Gently he leaned down and picked her up. She cuddled closer, still sound asleep as he carried her slowly up the stairs to her room and placed her on the folded comforter. She reached for him trustingly as he disentangled his arms from her sleep-warm hands.

Careful not to awaken her, he pulled the comforter up and tucked her in, then kissed her tenderly on the cheek and, surprised at himself, slipped from the darkened room.

Downstairs, Elaine had piled the cushions, the ones they'd used at their picnic, inside the door to the living room. In the light thrown into the garden by the open door at his back, David saw the quick flashes of fireflies among the bushes. Small rustles stirred through last year's fallen leaves, and in the distance the clear, loud trilling of a mockingbird rang out. Janice's presence filled the night, and David breathed deeply of the moist night air and thought of the woman lying sleeping in the room above. Her openness, her gentleness, and above all, her courage as she faced life alone with the two boys, made her somehow more real, more special.

The light behind him snapped off, and he broke off his thoughts. Elaine and he locked up and walked over to their cars. As Elaine climbed into her small sedan, she gave him a look that puzzled him. "Nine o'clock?" she said, raising an eyebrow questioningly.

He nodded and closed the door. But the look she'd given him stayed in his mind as her taillights vanished, cut off by the undergrowth. What had she meant by that look? For a moment she'd studied him, and her conclusions were still her own secret. He looked up at the dark windows, and they looked back at him, unwinkingly, giving away as little as Elaine had. How had he become involved with two such infuriatingly independent, fascinating women?

Just one short month ago, David would never have envisioned spending a Friday evening eating pizza on the floor, surrounded by a beautiful but exasperatingly uncooperative woman, her two young sons and a sharp-eyed chaperon. He shook his head in amazement as he walked over to his Jeep and drove off in low gear, alone. Alone—a short month ago he wouldn't have been alone unless he'd sought it. He felt unusually virtuous as he turned from under the overhanging trees onto the highway. His mind was made up. Regardless of the danger of involvement, knowing full well that he could genuinely be hurt for the first time in his adult life, he still had to pursue her.

Saturday morning the drought that had gripped the Washington area all year long broke. Janice yawned over her coffee and listened to the sound of distant thunder and rain pelting against the windows. The light outside was subdued, chastened by the varied shades of ominous gray rolling quickly across the sky. From the window, Janice could see the tops of the old oaks lining the drive whipping and bowing before the gusty wind. The different sounds of the house reacting to the fury of the outside elements demanded her attention, and she sat quietly, clothed in the warmth of her soft old jogging suit, listening. The rain hissed against the slate roof, creaks and groans issued from the woodwork, and a muffled clatter heralded a loose shutter in the other front bedroom.

Gradually Janice felt more at home, the new sounds taking their places in the song of the old house. With another yawn, determined not to miss any of this precious, quiet first morning, Janice stretched luxuriously and wandered through the unsettled rooms of her new house.

She felt at ease here, ghosting through these silent rooms in the shifting morning light. This weekend she had a lot of unpacking and arranging to do. She already had some ideas but was unable to concentrate on them. The half-remembered feel of David kissing her on the cheek, the security of being carried and cradled in his strong arms, the warm, soft beat of his heart next to her cheek, kept intruding.

What had happened to her pride? She thought she'd convinced herself that she couldn't afford to divide her attention between her sons and a lover. She'd tried. She thought she'd thrown him out, but David had shown up again as if nothing had happened. And she couldn't bring herself to be sorry.

A loud horn blasted, answered by the strangled squawking that announced Elaine's little import. Janice hurried to the front door as it rattled in a frantic tattoo. David stood dripping on the doorstep, arms laden with trash bags and an enormous tool kit. While Janice stood open-mouthed, staring at him, she was brushed aside by a swift-moving tangle of raincoat and the tantalizing smell of fresh doughnuts.

Elaine straightened up once she was out of the storm and shook the raincoat from her shoulders. "Ta-da," she cried, grinning as she thrust the boxes into Janice's hands. "Breakfast. Where's our coffee?"

Before Janice could respond, David's voice came from behind her. "Where are the boys?" He deposited his contributions beside the door and closed it against the driving rain. "Aren't they up yet? It's almost nine o'clock!" Suddenly he laughed, kissed the top of her head in passing and dashed for the stairs. "I'll get them up! Too much to do today for anyone to sleep late."

Janice was dazed. The quiet of the morning had vanished in a flash, but as she took Elaine through to the kitchen, she hid a delighted smile.

Chapter Seven

The weather was perfect, a typical June for Washington, sandwiched between the cold, wet spring and the miserable, humid furnace of August that was yet to come. David idled at the open window of the construction trailer, watching the glass being put into the skylights of the community center. These days, buildings could go up almost overnight, and in three more weeks he would be moving into the office his company would maintain in Riverbend Park until it was completely developed. This phase of a job always depressed him, and the weather wasn't enough to cheer him up. The first parcel of lots had already been sold to builders, and once the roads were completed in Area A, the houses would begin to go up.

"Then we'll go ahead with those blue tiles instead... Say, David, aren't you listening?" A large hand clapped him on the shoulder, and he turned around with a sigh. "Man, what's wrong with you? You've been dragging around here for the past week."

"Nothing really, Phil. Come on, I'll pay attention." David bent over the drafting table that held the spec sheet and tried to concentrate. "And what the hell does it matter if the bathrooms have blue or white tiles, anyway?"

Phil, his foreman, was taken aback at this sudden rejoinder. He frowned, his bushy eyebrows bristling aggressively. "Hell, I don't know. You're the one who was so upset when these were delivered!" He leaned against the wall and puffed furiously on his half-lit cigar. "Seriously, pal, why don't you get out in the fresh air. You've been cooped up in here for days now, and to tell you the truth, we'll do a lot better without you looking over our shoulders." His eyes narrowed. "Go on, leave. Go take a look at our Janice. She's a sight for sore eyes!"

David's lips tightened, and his eyes narrowed dangerously. The very mention of Janice's name infuriated him, and to hear Phil talking so affectionately about her was more than he could take.

Phil didn't see the effect his words had on his boss as he'd already turned back to the drafting table. "She's done wonders for morale at this job," he continued. "You should see her today—dynamite legs!" He turned his head, but David was abruptly gone, leaving the trailer door practically humming from his passage.

Blindly, not seeing the newly completed walkways winding around the community center or noticing the golden June day, David stormed past the busy work crews, his mind fixed on his failure. Ever since the weekend of the move, Janice had managed to keep their relationship on a friendly footing. He'd been a regular visitor, practically one of the family, taking the boys riding and hiking. But for two weeks he'd made no headway with their mother.

Sure, he was getting to know her better, and liked her more each day, but that wasn't enough. She had begun to obsess him. In frustration he'd called Patricia. They'd done all the right things—gone out to dinner, a play and ended up in her apartment—but he hadn't been interested and had left after one drink, pleading an early morning at the job. Patricia had been furious. Even her anger hadn't moved him.

David slammed his fist against a tree trunk. It shook, dropping a few withered leaves at his feet. He looked up. He was standing by one of the dogwoods just moved from Janice's old property. With a bitter laugh, he backed away. That woman, she was everywhere. And the worst of it was that he could tell she was just as attracted to him as he was to her. Every time he was near her, or touched her hand, or even spoke to her, he could sense the passion seething under her iron control.

Why did she insist upon denying him? If two adults wanted each other, why not? Neither had other obligations.

But, David thought angrily, that wasn't so, was it? Although Janice's husband had been gone for two

years, she regarded herself as a widow and as the
mother of two young children. But that shouldn't
make any difference, he fumed. The boys shouldn't
be his rivals—nothing could or should interfere with
her love for them—and he shouldn't have to com-
pete with them, either.

"Hey, lady. How's it going?"

A loud call from a passing truck broke into his
troubled thoughts, and his eyes focused on movement in the shrubs along the stream. Janice straightened up, shaking her hair back from her forehead,
and waved at the sun-burned workmen on their way
to grade the winding roads of the community. She
looked relaxed and at ease, with a trowel in one
gloved hand and a tray of flowering annuals in the
other. One of the passing men whistled as she turned
back to her work.

David was appalled at the rush of fury that overwhelmed him, and he literally ran back the way he'd
come, slammed into his Jeep and drove off in a
writhing cloud of red dust. He didn't go far. His in-
ternal anguish stopped him just down the road where
the old E & J Garden Center had been.

But nothing was the same. All the flowering dogwoods and azaleas were gone, and the parking lot
they'd framed looked forlorn and bleak, surrounded by the gaping holes they'd inhabited. The
greenhouses had been dismantled, and the old farm-
house looked naked without its glass adornment.
David thought about the first time he'd driven up
here before he'd met Janice. With a shock, he realized how much his life had changed since that mo-

ment he'd first seen her. He was miserable because of that woman. All his self-confidence seemed to have disappeared, leaving him incomplete, unsure.

"That's it!" David pounded his clenched hands against the wheel. "She's not worth it!" Feeling immediately better for having vented his frustration, David turned back to the site, striving to ignore Janice as he picked up the pieces of his existence and got back to work.

That evening he called Patricia again.

Janice had been watching David warily from a safe distance. For days he'd been ignoring her, speaking only when work brought them together, and then sharply. With a pang of regret, she thought how tired he looked today, wrung out, dark shadows under his eyes and lines of strain around his tight mouth.

Miserably she knew that his new, sullen mood stemmed from her own insistence on keeping him at arm's length. The knowledge that she was responsible didn't help her ease her loneliness and hurt, however, and her own mood had suffered as a consequence. It didn't help, either, to point out to herself that his pique just proved she was right. They wanted different things from life. He was unmarried, uncommitted, unfettered; she had a family and responsibilities. But even with this bitter consolation, Janice missed him desperately. She missed the tension, the excitement of his obvious desire, the tenderness he so often showed, the sound of his ready laughter in the company of her sons, and yes, the thrill that quivered along her entire body whenever they were together, whenever they touched.

Janice snapped out of her preoccupation as David strode in her direction. She looked around, but there was no one else nearby and no handy reason to avoid him, so she braced herself for another confrontation.

"Why isn't that picnic area sodded over yet?" His voice was impersonal, harsh and unyielding. "You're two days behind schedule already." He folded his arms and glared at her.

Unexpected rage welled in her, and she clenched her teeth to avoid screaming with fury. This was one time too many. With icy control, Janice responded, "You know the reason for the delay as well as I do—unless you don't read your own memos." Stiffly she walked to her portfolio, took out the relevant memo and thrust it angrily into his hands.

David looked taken aback. He'd actually forgotten, forgotten his own memo, Janice realized, and her rage redoubled.

"In future, if you have a problem with me," Janice said furiously, her voice rising, "I would appreciate it if you would take it up with me privately. Don't let personal differences interfere with business." Without waiting to see his reaction, she stalked angrily to her car and drove off. As she turned onto the highway, she saw him still standing, memo in hand, and her rage disappeared in bitter laughter.

How foolish, she thought. They were both behaving like children, but even realizing this, she couldn't bring herself to return to the site that day. Childish or not, the past few days had been rough. David's foul mood and her own touchiness had thrown sparks more than once. She needed a break and drove home through the glorious rolling hills, the natural beauty of the farms and rising foothills easing her mind.

Tired, but almost calm again, Janice turned her car up the drive. She sat, watching the work in progress on the old barn before driving up to the house. She climbed out of the car and walked back down the driveway. The play of light through the overhanging leaves dappled the newly graded drive, forming a kaleidoscope of patterns. The swirl and change of the diffused sunlight rested her, helping her to overcome the tension raised by David's mood. She lingered, taking her time walking under the soothing shade of the oak trees, their lush summer foliage forming a luminous green roof overhead. The air under the arching greenery was fresh and invigorating, washing away the last of the irritation that had plagued her.

She stood under the shadows and watched the activity. The new E & J Garden Center was well under way. Elaine stood with the builder, poring over the detailed plans David had drawn up. Janice knew the drawings by heart. The concrete foundations had been poured almost two weeks earlier, and the framework of the shop/greenhouse was nearly complete. By the end of the week, the structure would probably be ready to receive the glass that would enclose an entire half of the old barn and some of the shop area. The wooden slats for the floors were stacked beside the leftover stones. David had made use of those weather-beaten stones for walls, arches and pillars that would bind the contemporary building design with the archaic beauty of the hundred-year-old ruin. Janice could already visualize the airy, earthy, delicate structure, with its contradictory elements of stone and glass.

It would take time to settle into the new premises. Janice could hardly wait to begin stocking the greenhouse and arranging the outdoor shrubbery she'd ordered from the wholesaler. Next year, she'd be able to plant her own shrubs and would no longer have to rely on outside suppliers. That was the bonus that had come with this new location.

She'd missed her late-evening inspections of the greenhouses, the solitude, the free rein she found for her dreams in the misty silence.

How time changed people, she thought in sudden amazement. Before she'd met Jay, she'd spent her whole life in intellectual surroundings, never dirtying her hands in the earth, or even realizing that a way of life not dependent upon the university could exist. Over the years, she'd become more involved with the realities of living—nothing like a child with the flu to bring you down to earth, she thought with a laugh.

"Where were you just now?" Elaine's amused voice sounded at her side. "I've been trying to catch your attention for five minutes at least!" She took Janice by the elbow and led her toward the low stone wall outlining the new center, "What do you think?"

Not waiting for a reply, she continued enthusiastically, "It's going to be beautiful, isn't it? Look at the rich colors of those old stones! And here," she said, pointing to a level, graded area beyond the barn's foundations, "this whole area will be gravel and mulch. Here's where we'll keep the azaleas and other shrubs."

The two women strolled happily around the site, comparing it with the old garden center. "It was nice of David to find the house and do the designs for the garden center, wasn't it?" Elaine felt Janice stiffen at the mention of his name and looked sharply at her. Her friend was frowning, tense, unhappy. "Okay, what's wrong?" Elaine asked as they walked up the drive. "You two have barely been speaking to each other for the past two weeks. What's happened?" She raised her eyebrow at Janice's look of shocked surprise. "Oh, come on, it's been perfectly obvious that something went wrong. What's the latest?"

Janice gave a strained laugh. "I should have known nothing could be hidden from you." Her eyes looked everywhere but at her friend. "Honestly, I'd tell you if I could, Elaine. Today he raved about being behind schedule on the sod for the picnic area when we all know the reason for that delay." She laughed nervously. "I'm afraid I gave him a hard time about it."

"Well, good for you. That man's been asking for it. He's been acting like a spoiled child for weeks now."

"Hasn't he just!"

They walked on in silence until the house came into sight.

Elaine shook her head. "Well, you've got my sympathy, kiddo. But if you figure out anything that will bring him out of this mood, let me know."

As they rounded the corner of the house, Janice felt her blush deepen and hurried to escape Elaine's sharp-eyed attention. "I've really got to fix this up," she mumbled, pulling ineffectually at the tangled honeysuckle wrapped around the sundial.

Elaine was just too sharp sometimes, Janice mused as she dressed for work the next morning. She wished she could confide in her, but she didn't know what she felt or wanted. She wasn't even sure if anything worth mentioning had happened between them. Thank goodness Elaine would be at Riverbend this morning. Another day under David's glowering visage was more than she could stand at the moment. But at least Elaine would be there. *She* could handle him!

The day started badly. When Janice arrived at Riverbend Park, the sound of angry voices spilled out of the open windows of the construction trailer. She quailed as she heard David and Elaine actually yelling at each other. Was the entire world going mad?

Before she could retreat, Elaine came slamming out of the trailer, pale with anger, her mouth a thin line of disapproval. She saw Janice and made a visible effort to control her agitated breathing.

"Let's go get some coffee, Janice." She glanced back at the trailer as she hurried her partner to the parking lot. "Come on. I'll tell you all about it when we get there."

As they drove off, Elaine lit a cigarette and shrugged at Janice's questioning look. "Just one. He made me so angry. I need something to calm me down."

Whether or not it was the cigarette, Elaine was beginning to relax by the time they pulled into Manny's Pancake House fifteen minutes later. They sat in a corner booth shaded from the morning sun by handwoven Mexican curtains and drank the surprisingly good coffee Manny roasted and ground for special customers.

Janice allowed Elaine to sit in silence for a while. Then, as she watched the tension drain from her friend, her curiosity got the best of her. "Well?"

"Wow!" Elaine looked up with a wry grin on her face. "Why didn't you warn me? He's worse than a rogue elephant." Janice burst out laughing at the vision of David stampeding through the flower beds. At first, Elaine was shocked at Janice's laughter. "It's not funny!" she protested. But as her friend continued to laugh helplessly, unable to explain, she succumbed to Janice's infectious gaiety.

Wiping the hint of tears from her eyes, Elaine sighed heavily and leaned back with her coffee. "Oh, I needed that. But I meant what I said. He's not the same person he was two weeks ago. I just don't understand it. Now he's decided he doesn't like the entire landscape design that he approved just a month ago!''

Janice gasped. But he'd loved that design! She remembered his enthusiasm as she was making the preliminary sketches, his continual delight in the way her drawings brought his visions for the community to life. The whole thing? She couldn't believe it.

She'd put her best, her heart and soul, into those plans. For one wild moment she wondered if David were doing this on purpose to hurt her. But that was impossible. She'd thought they'd come to an understanding after the first fight when she'd sent him away. Since then, he'd started the boys' riding lessons, taken them all hiking and helped them complete their move into the new house. Sure, she'd kept her distance, but he'd seemed to have accepted it.

What had changed him? Or had she completely misread him from the beginning? Through her mind there flashed that picture—the way she'd first seen him on television. The kindness, the charm, the physical attraction of that moment—he truly had all of these qualities. She'd seen them in him since. What was now showing up was one more facet of the stranger she'd confronted in her kitchen. It reminded her forcibly that whatever she thought she knew of him was based on a superficial acquaintance, despite the intimacy of their kiss that night under the stars.

Her eyes, tragic from the loss of that night's magic, lifted to meet her partner's. ''What did you say to him?''

"Well," Elaine said with an attempt at humor, "I won't tell you word for word, but basically I told him what he could do with his objections."

"You didn't!" Janice looked horrified. "Oh, Elaine!" She giggled, visualizing Elaine and David, two strong-minded people, in a toe-to-toe confrontation.

They ordered more coffee and settled down to a serious discussion of the problem. "Frankly, Janice, I told him I was thinking of pulling out of the contract, and I think we ought to. If we continue, do we redesign, or do we insist upon the original design? After all, that was the design the contract was based on. If we have to change that—particularly now—when we've already begun, we'll lose plants and end up working a month beyond schedule. That'll put us in the red."

"I won't transplant those azaleas. And the bedding plants won't take a move either." Janice lapsed into a glum silence. Then, coming to a decision, she spoke up. "You're right, Elaine. If he insists upon a major change in the design, we'll have to cancel. Can we get payment for the work we've already done?"

"Well, it's not at that point yet," Elaine said firmly. "The first thing to do is to talk to David, tomorrow." She laughed. "E & J Garden Center is closed for the day!"

Much later they paid for the coffee and walked out into the sunlight, blinking in the sudden brightness. "Say," Elaine suggested on the spur of the moment, "let's really take the day off. There's a new restaurant open at Fair Oaks Mall. I'll treat you to lunch, and then we'll go spend a fortune on something we don't need!''

Janice looked at her friend doubtfully for a moment, then, shaking off her guilt at leaving a job half-finished, she said, "Great idea! Just what we need! I'll even get the boys those fire trucks they've been after me to buy."

Feeling as though they were playing hooky, the two women set off down the highway.

At four o'clock that afternoon, Janice and Elaine drove back to Riverbend Park in their new finery. Packages littered the back seat, and both women were feeling much more relaxed after a leisurely lunch and a bottle of wine. The trucks for the boys were hidden in the trunk. Janice looked forward to hiding them in the house among the last few boxes waiting to be unpacked.

Elaine doubtfully regarded the white leather shoes she'd bought to match her new suit of white linen with the royal blue braid trim. "Maybe I should take these back," she said. "I've never worn heels as high as these before." She slipped them on, looking from their delicate lines to the uneven surface of the packed earth around the construction trailer. She shrugged. "Oh, well. Can't wear clogs with this outfit." She stood up, teetering to find her balance.

"Careful," Janice spluttered, trying hard not to laugh at the wolf whistles that greeted them. "Are you sure you want to confront him today?"

"Yes," she answered. "I want to get this over with." She sent an exaggerated glare in the general direction of the offending sounds and turned to wink at Janice. Then, tossing her head, she squared her shoulders. "Here goes," she said. Suddenly serious, all humor wiped from her face and voice, she asked, "Still sure?" Janice nervously twisted her hair but nodded resolutely. Elaine walked carefully erect over to the trailer and climbed the cinder-block steps.

David was seated at his desk, irritably reworking his latest balance sheet. His hair was rumpled, his tie thrown over the back of another chair, and his shirt-sleeves rolled up to his elbows. He looked up and frowned as Elaine came in, then put down his ruler and stood.

"Where have you been?" he demanded testily, echoing the question he'd been asked every other minute during the entire day. Apparently everyone involved in the construction of Riverbend took a lively interest in the two women and had missed them.

Elaine said nothing, crossing to the desk in silence.

Lips tight, David indicated a chair, but she ignored his offer. "Mr. Phillips," Elaine said, formally correct. "I've been discussing this job with my partner. Our original design, based upon your specifications and descriptions, was written into the contract. The job cost, the schedule, every detail was vetted by Mr. Hanrahan and your lawyers before we signed the contract."

David felt himself go pale. Why was she talking so formally about lawyers? The pencil he was holding snapped with the crack of a rifle shot in the still pause before she spoke again.

"E & J Garden Center wants to complete this contract. Therefore, my partner and I will be agreeable to minor modifications of the plans before the work on that specific area has begun. These modifications must be approved in writing and attached to the original contract." Coolly Elaine noted that David was more upset then she'd expected him to be, barely maintaining his controlled facade. Elaine hesitated, feeling as though she were betraying a friend, then continued, "However, the changes you requested this morning are radical and involve recently transplanted trees and shrubs that will not take kindly to being moved again." Her eyes locked onto his. "If you insist, Mr. Phillips, we will withdraw and give you the names of other garden centers that might be willing to take over the work."

David sagged into his chair, his behavior over the past few weeks flashing through his mind. Had he really been as unpleasant as all that? Never before had his personal life interfered with his business, but lately he seemed to have lost all control. Elaine watched as all David's bravado drained, leaving him looking curiously vulnerable. His eyes were looking somewhere far away. Finally he took a deep breath and said in a quiet, remarkably chastened voice, "Elaine—please drop the 'Mr. Phillips.'"

He stood. "I don't know what's got into me lately. I can't explain it. But I thought we were friends. I want us to be friends. I don't want to lose that." He offered his hand. "Please forgive my bad temper. Let's pretend the last two weeks never happened and settle everything over dinner."

Relieved but suspicious, Elaine's cold expression and tense stance relaxed. She let him stand with hand outstretched as she considered his apology. She'd never known him to be other than sincere and honest. His eyes now met hers directly, and she nodded, convinced finally that his change of heart was real. She took his hand gladly. "I'm glad you've snapped out of that." With a challenging smile, she pressed her luck. "I take it those major modifications have been dropped?"

He squeezed her hand and gave an embarrassed laugh. "If I ever mention changes again, even moving a bulb, you have my permission to throw me in the river—shoes, jacket and all." Lighthearted, free of the depression that had hemmed him in for so long, David leaned across the desk and looked down at Elaine's four-inch heels. "Talking about change, you can take those shoes off now. The eye-to-eye confrontation is over!"

Relieved, they laughed together, pleased to be back on a friendly footing again. Elaine turned to leave the trailer while David collected his jacket and tie before following.

He didn't get far. As he stepped through the open door, his heart rose as he heard Janice laughing excitedly. He looked toward her and went cold.

Janice's graceful, passionate body was crushed in the embrace of a young, handsome, laughing man. Her arms clung tightly around his neck, her shapely legs visible as they strained to lift her to his embrace. Their cheeks were pressed together, and as David watched in sick horror, the young stranger lifted her from the ground and swung her around in a joyful swirl.

Elaine's grip in his arm barely registered as she turned toward him, smiling broadly. He didn't see her. He could see nothing but the disaster unfolding in his life. It seemed, all at once, so terribly clear how important this woman was to him, how devastating her loss would be. Shock after shock rippled strongly through him as so many things became clear.

Jealousy—the clashes of the past few weeks arose from jealousy! Him? Jealous?

He loved Janice. The realization astounded him.

She was the one woman who fit the future as he envisaged it. Everything about her was right for him. He remembered the feel of her body in the moonlight—how every curve, every part of her had fitted in his arms. He recalled her lively interest, the delight of discovering her shared feelings about nature, living and growth. The way she acted with her sons—able to participate in their enthusiasms yet be firm when necessary—was the way he would want to be with his own children.

Elaine watched the emotions and thoughts play across David's face. With intuitive understanding of her own, she read the story of his feelings as he lived them. She saw clearly his recognition of the all-encompassing love he felt for Janice. Suddenly his whole body shuddered, as though an electric shock of great force had ripped through him.

His face, which had been softened by his love, contorted for an instant into rage. Elaine grabbed him, yanked him up the steps into the trailer and thrust him, with a strength she didn't know she had, into a chair.

It seemed forever to her before she saw him focus on her. Her voice was low and urgent as she tried to calm him and make him understand. Finally his eyes cleared, and he saw her and heard what she was saying.

"... brother-in-law. They've always been very close. She helped Jay raise him after their parents died."

David gaped at her. "What?"

"It's Randy Haley, her brother-in-law." She stopped.

For the second time that day, David felt the tension drain as though a plug had been pulled. He found himself staring unseeingly at Elaine and blinked himself alert. "Her brother-in-law?" he asked numbly.

As the welcome truth sank in, David began to laugh softly, feeling that if he let himself go he'd never be able to stop. It was all right. He had another chance. Another chance to reach for the happiness he knew they could have together.

He felt like a new man. The cloud that had been haunting him for weeks had vanished in the face of Elaine's revelation. He hugged Elaine quickly. "Introduce me."

He walked out into the late-afternoon shadows, followed by a flustered Elaine patting her hair back into place. Janice turned, her face lit with pleasure, the irritation between them forgotten.

"Elaine, look. David, come and meet Randy."

David looked at Randy. He was deeply tanned, his eyes crinkled as though he spent his time squinting against a bright sun. His smile was quick and disarming. David stepped forward, hand outstretched, his own face relaxing into welcome.

Chapter Eight

David collapsed on the hard wooden bench of the locker room and watched as Randy Haley carefully wiped and put away his graphite tennis racket.

Hands on hips, Randy turned to David. With a challenging gleam in his eye, he asked teasingly, "What's wrong with you? It's only eighty-six degrees out there. You look like you've been roasted."

"Sure, go ahead and laugh! You don't have to work all day. You're on vacation." He tossed his drenched towel into his bag and zipped it closed. "I was on the site at six this morning, and you were still snoring at ten. What kind of working hours have they got out there in Saudi Arabia, anyway?" He slammed the door of his locker with his foot and stood up. "I'm parched. How about a drink?"

"Well," Randy said, grinning, "just to keep you company..."

The two men made their way from the locker room to the country club's patio. As they parked their bags on the floor and relaxed in the shade of the red-and-blue awning, the waiter came over. "Good afternoon, Mr. Phillips, Mr. Haley. Who's buying today?"

David laughed. "I am—who do you think? This guy should be at Wimbledon. At least poor saps like me would have some warning then."

"The usual?" At David's nod, the waiter left them, returning shortly with the ice-cold beer and a bowl of peanuts.

Although it was eight o'clock, it was still light outside. Long shadows of pine and maple trees slanted across the rich green fairway. As they sipped their beer, the patio and bar began to fill up with golfers coming off the course.

David watched, amused as Randy appreciatively eyed a young woman across the room, who was obviously just as interested in him. She had blond shoulder-length hair, a lithe body and long legs which were tanned and muscular under her short golf skirt. Leaning forward, David said, "Her name's Devon Richardson. She's the reigning golf champion at the club. Would you like to meet her?"

Randy looked over at David assessingly. "Good friend of yours, huh?"

"Well," David said, rather taken aback at the question, "we went through Sunday school together. And we've known each other all our lives."

To his surprise, Randy looked acutely embarrassed, his eyes refusing to meet David's. As David puzzled over Randy's reaction, Devon, who'd watched the byplay, sauntered over to the two men. David stood, followed quickly by Randy, and she stepped close, hugged one arm around David's waist and kissed his cheek.

"Hullo, Dave. Who's your friend?"

David caught the look on Randy's face; it made his previous question clear. "Hello, Devon. May I introduce Randy Haley? Devon Richardson." The two shook hands across the table, and Randy felt the extra pressure that, coupled with a flirtatious sideways glimpse of her teasing eyes through long eyelashes, told him a great deal about David's childhood friend.

Perfectly able to play the game with her, Randy hung on to her hand. "Will you join us? It's David's night to buy."

Devon laughed provocatively and turned an innocent, wide-eyed gaze upon the man still standing at her side. "How nice, he's always so generous." She shook her head at the approaching waiter. "Thanks, Randy, but I really can't stay." She waved at someone across the room. "So," she almost seemed to purr as she focused the full force of her attention on Randy, "will you be around for a while?"

"Only another two weeks, I'm afraid. I'm just visiting my family. However," he murmured, "I've always got time for a lovely woman."

"Oh," Devon said, moving away from David, "then perhaps I should challenge you to a game. Tennis?" She cocked an eyebrow at him. "Day after tomorrow—six o'clock?"

"Enchanted." Randy raised her hand to his lips, brushing her long, slender fingers with a light kiss. "Six o'clock," he whispered against her skin.

Amused, David watched Devon play her games. Randy, he saw, was not taken in. Rather, he was playing along with her. And very slickly, too, he thought, as he watched the final maneuvering.

Looking sheepish but triumphant, Randy met David's eyes. "That's what I like about the States. Life is a lot simpler here."

David grinned sympathetically. "That's Devon all right."

"Yes," Randy said in a peculiar, thoughtful tone. He was thinking of Janice. "That's *Devon* all right." He looked consideringly at David. "If you play by her rules, she'll never get hurt."

David looked over at him in surprise. His eyes narrowed. "Hold it," he said. "What's that supposed to mean?" They sat down to their beers again. "If you've got something to say to me, come right out with it."

"Okay." Randy slowly poured out the last of his beer. "Okay, straight out." He met David's eye. "It's about Janice. I care very deeply for her and for the boys, and you puzzle me."

David was taken aback by Randy's reply, and for a moment he looked curiously vulnerable. Then,

rallying himself, he changed the subject and said,
"I'm starved. How about dinner?"

Frustrated by David's evasion, but relieved that
the difficult subject could be avoided a bit longer,
Randy stood. "Where shall we go?"

"Well, if you don't mind, let's eat here. On Tues-
days, the special is barbecued ribs, and the chef has
his own special recipe that's won awards throughout
Virginia." He scraped his chair back and picked up
his bag. "Let's leave these in the car so we don't have
to worry about them."

The twilight was deepening as they came back to
the clubhouse and made their way to the glassed-in
dining room. The louvered glass panes were open,
and a fresh breeze brought a faint scent of honeysuckle with it. The lake and boathouse were visible
through the thin screen of trees, and the lights on the
dock glimmered across the water. Beyond, the
mountains were etched black against the sunset,
which lingered, throwing muted colors onto a few
scattered low-lying clouds.

David and Randy found a corner table overlooking part of the lake and the distantly lit tennis courts.
Within minutes, crisp salads were served, a new
round of cold beer was before them, and the aroma
of the ribs gave promise of a memorable dinner to
come.

"Look," David began after they were settled, "I
think I can understand why you're concerned, and I
can't say I blame you." He took a slow sip of beer.
"If I hadn't come to like you over the past two
weeks, I wouldn't explain myself no matter what

your reasons for asking." The waiter arrived with a basket of hot, fresh bread and extra napkins.

Randy shifted uneasily. How he wished he didn't have to listen to this, but his concern and feeling of responsibility for his sister-in-law demanded it. Funny, he thought, how their roles seemed to have reversed. Janice had helped him through late adolescence and into his twenties, treating him like a younger brother, or even an older son. Now it was his turn. Nothing—no one—would hurt her or Jay's sons if he could help it. He gritted his teeth, lit a cigarette and prepared to listen.

David's tone was reminiscent, fond, as if of a treasured memory. "I think Janice is the most wonderful, most interesting woman I've ever met. I didn't realize I was in love with her until the day you arrived." His eyes glittered across the table at Randy. "When I saw Janice in your arms, I could have killed you." He smiled mischievously. "It was close—I tell you, it was very close.

"That moment was an eye-opener," he said, serious again. "It forced me to acknowledge that she means more to me than anyone else ever has." He grinned wryly. "And those boys... I'd always thought that somewhere down the line I'd get married and have kids—later—when I was thirty-five or so. But, it's happened to me now." He shook his head. "I never anticipated anyone like Janice. And now I've fallen in love with her and her two sons."

Randy couldn't help laughing. David looked so helpless, quite unlike the person Randy knew him to be. He remembered their first meeting and the tall, self-possessed man who'd scrutinized him. Since then, he'd come to admire David immensely. He'd seen him at work, playing with the boys, intently following the course of a small brown bird through distant courtship rites, or wrapped in an apron, flour on his hands, helping Janice make fresh strawberry pie. He'd always exuded self-confidence. Until now.

David frowned. "Just wait till it happens to you. The laugh you hear in the background will be mine." He couldn't keep a straight face any longer and joined in Randy's laughter.

The waiter smiled to see them enjoying themselves so much and placed a steaming dish of ribs on the table.

As Randy reached for the ribs, David said, "We only met a couple of months ago, you know. It's kind of frightening..." His voiced trailed off, and Randy nodded. Randy understood. He'd had one close brush with love himself, but unlike this man he'd come to think of as his friend, he'd never had the chance to declare himself.

Neither spoke further until the last of the ribs had been eaten, fingers rinsed in the bowls and coffee ordered.

"It's funny," David said musingly, idly stirring sugar into his cup, "but at times it all seems unreal—as if I were dreaming. I barely know her. And yet," he added with a warm, inward-looking smile, "every new thing I learn just fits somehow, so perfectly." He shook his head. "Sometimes I'm afraid that if I make one wrong step it'll all disappear."

Randy watched David, suddenly understanding all the things that had puzzled him. It was pretty obvious to anyone watching David and Janice that they had a mutual fascination for each other. Each seemed hypersensitive to the other's presence, aware of the other's movements through the house, as though there were some invisible cord linking them. Randy had watched, unobserved. He'd never seen them touch or kiss or evidence any feeling other than liking and easy companionship. Yet he'd been aware of hidden tensions lurking somewhere.

But why should David be so worried that everything could disappear?

Randy wondered if Janice simply didn't see David's yearning. Or, if she did see it, was she afraid? She'd become a different person since Jay's death. During the past two years, she'd had to cope with things Jay had always seen to. Randy knew how hard it must have been for her to stand alone—Janice wasn't made to be solitary. He thought about her affectionately. Yes, David just might be right for her.

It was late when they left the country club. As they separated, each heading for his own car, David remembered his message. "Oh, by the way, would you remind the boys to be ready at 5:30 tomorrow night?"

Randy nodded. "Sure." He grinned. "It's not really necessary, you know. Jonathan keeps moving his boots to the front door where everyone trips over them."

"Does he?" David laughed. "He's going to be a good rider someday," he added.

* * *

With the high energy of youth, the boys were playing in the back seat as David drove them home after their lesson the next day. He wished he still had that kind of energy, but even though he'd been riding all his life, an hour's training was hard work. Teaching was easier on the muscles, but, oh, his throat was dry from calling instructions across the ring. He hoped Janice would offer him a long, cold drink—seeing her was the bonus he got for ferrying the boys to and from their lessons.

He turned up the drive. On the left, he could see that the greenhouse framework was now filled in with glass and that the skylights in the shop roof were in place. So soon, he thought. They should be able to open for business by the end of the month. And by then, Riverbend Park's landscaping should be completed. Almost grimly, David realized he was coming up against a deadline. If he wasn't able to find a comfortable niche in her life by then, it would become much more difficult to approach her.

"How did it go?" Janice called to the boys from the front door. "You certainly look like you had fun. What a mess! Leave your boots at the back door and take a shower. Lemonade's all ready on the porch." As the boys scampered around the side of the house, she smiled fondly at them, then turned back. "Hello, David. Come on in. There's some cold beer in the fridge. I'm sorry Randy's not here. He had a date with an old girlfriend of his." She avoided his eyes and straightened the pillows on the rocking chair. "Do sit down," she chattered. "I'll get the beer."

David hid an amused smile. Janice's fidgeting was a dead giveaway. That one night—he glanced toward the back steps—was not forgotten, would never be forgotten, if he could help it. He took her hands and pretended not to notice her reaction to his touch. It felt so good to be touching her again, even if only to feel her trembling fingers in his own. "Sit down, Janice. I know where the beer is." He pointed her toward the sofa and went to the kitchen.

He loved this house. Janice had made it friendly and welcoming. Every time he walked through the door, he felt at ease, even though his relationship with Janice wasn't particularly easy at the moment. The creative talent that she used to such good effect in her landscaping took another direction in her home. The furniture and pictures, for example, were the same she'd had in the old house, but here her motley collection of antiques and comfortable chairs looked entirely different. The yellowed wallpaper in the living room had been replaced, the fireplace had been cleaned in preparation for use, and mismatched blinds had been added to complete the picture. Rather than feeling chaotic, the room was relaxing and accommodating.

Every room in the house was obviously meant to be lived in. Books and toys were ever present but not allowed to get out of hand. Most of the walls had Janice's favorite drawings in small clusters, but there were still vast areas of empty space. As he returned to the porch, David thought about how nice his watercolor painting of the indigo bunting would look over the fireplace.

Janice was no longer on the porch when David returned. As the light faded over the hills, he stood and listened to the evening song of the mockingbird. Even though the bird was out of sight, its powerful voice sent the varied song into the twilight. David listened raptly as it chirped and warbled, imitating cardinals, blue jays and finches. From above, he heard the faint sounds of boyish laughter and their mother's admonishments to hurry as her footsteps descended the stairs.

David could smell the subtle, light perfume Janice wore even before she came out onto the porch, and he clenched his fists to keep himself from going to her, from taking her in his arms and perhaps scaring her away forever.

"How are the boys doing?" she asked. "They love riding, you know."

He heard her sit down, and soft lamplight spilled onto the floor around his feet as he turned. Janice's delicate features were edged by shadow as she leaned back in the rocking chair. Her eyes looked enormous in the light thrown by the lamp, and David yearned to have the right to go to her, to change her troubled expression to one of confidence, laughter and passion. Her eyes questioned him now, and he had to think for a moment to recall the question. "Oh, they're both doing very well. Jason works very hard at learning, and Jonathan is a natural rider. If they keep it up, you might want to consider buying them horses in a few years." He drained his beer. "Why don't you let me teach you to ride?" As she looked at him in astonishment, he grinned and said, "Why not? I think you'd love it."

"Perhaps," she said, amused at his enthusiasm.

"If you'd learn, we could all go out on trail rides. It'd be great." His smile, while still lazily friendly, no longer reflected the intensity of his eyes, which were glowing, compelling her to remember the joy she'd found in his arms.

Janice tried to wrench her gaze away. Why did he still affect her so? Would she ever be free of him? Did she truly want to be? If only she were the kind of woman who could take pleasure where she found it.

David made a sudden movement, reaching toward her, and Janice jumped. She rose swiftly from the chair to hide her blush. How long had they been entranced like that? The sound of the summer cicadas and a few night birds calling seemed loud in contrast to that extended moment in which their eyes had locked.

The moment was broken, and the clatter of the boys' feet on the stairs brought relief from the tension. "David, David!" With Jonathan close at his heels, Jason threw himself across the porch. "Can I ride Kip next time? Please."

Jonathan chimed in, "And I want to ride Poco. Can I, please?" The two boys circled around him excitedly, and David's face was alight as he responded.

Janice, in the shadow of the living room, watched her sons and the tall man who had become part of all their lives. *If only...* She turned to go to the kitchen, throat tight with conflicting emotions. Over her shoulder she asked, "Will you stay for spaghetti? It'll be ready in just a few minutes."

"Yes, please!" the boys echoed in support.

"How could I refuse?" he said laughing. As always, being a part of this family brought a glow of warmth that made him want to stay forever. Each time it was harder to leave. Soon, he promised himself, watching Janice retreat to the kitchen, soon he would no longer have to leave when the boys went to bed. She was beginning to relax around him again, allowing the desire underlying her fear to show.

Janice was confused. It seemed to be a permanent state of mind for her recently. The moonlight made the curtains glow in the darkness of her room. She turned her back to the window, trying to cut out memories of another moonlit night as she closed her eyes determinedly. If she couldn't get to sleep soon, she'd be exhausted tomorrow when she would need all her wits for overseeing the laying of sod at Riverbend Park. The last of the job, she thought, her eyes opening against her will.

David... She wouldn't see him every day then. His presence on the site wouldn't make her nerves come alive anymore. He'd come around to pick up the boys and drop them off, and eventually even that contact would fail. Janice turned over. A light breeze stirred the curtains, and a shaft of moonlight fell across her bed. It would be for the best, she thought with empty despair. Then she would no longer be torn between her desires and what was right.

It took a long time for Janice to find sleep, and when she did, it was light, fitful and full of foreboding. Yet, underlying it all was a rising hope that all her strength couldn't subdue—he had, after all, kept coming back. With a persistence that she was beginning to admire, David was wearing down her defenses. Each time he was near her she got weaker, less able to keep him at arm's length. Already he came and went at will with the boys, and she couldn't refuse their enthusiastic plans for sailing, hiking and swimming.

Even Randy seemed to like David well enough, Janice thought resentfully. Of course, they were the same age. She turned onto her back and stared at the ceiling. The same age—four years younger than she was—it didn't seem so much when you said it that way. Neither one of them had ever been married, however, and that was the true difference. Whenever Randy came to visit, he was great with his nephews, just as David was. But playing with nephews is vastly different from having your own children with you day in and day out, night in and night out. No, she thought to herself, Randy was still not ready for his own family and made no pretensions of being ready. Nor, she told herself, was David. He was still very much single, and she'd been married even before she'd had the chance to live alone. How could she ever understand him, or he her?

Dawn finally lightened the sky, and Janice slid from under the sheet. She felt light, pithless, as though the sleepless night had purged her of solidity. Another day to be spent under the shadow of her confusion.

As she arrived on the site, eyes aching from lack of sleep, the storm clouds moved in over the hills, and the rain began to fall. Janice ran for cover to the community center, and, holding a cup of coffee, looked out through the sheets of water sliding down the floor-to-ceiling windows. Already puddles were forming in the areas prepared for the sod.

David came up behind her. She could see his reflection in the mirror of the water as he approached and put an arm around her shoulder. "Looks like we have the day off. Even if it lets up now, your sod will have to wait." He loosened his tie. "I'll be glad to have a day off for a change. Today was the day I was going to mark off the lots of Area D with the surveyors, but they don't work in weather like this." He tilted her chin and smiled into her eyes. "Let me drive you home," he said, stroking the hair from her forehead. "You look as though you could use the day off as much as I can."

David's touch melted Janice's tension, and she leaned gratefully into his support without worrying about any implications for a change. As he went off to inform his secretary and dismiss the men, she closed her eyes wearily. How good it was to have someone to care for you.

The smell of bacon frying met them at the door as they kicked off their wet shoes. "Hello," Janice called.

"We're out here, Mom," Jason answered from the porch.

"We're making breakfast," Jonathan's voice added. "Uncle Randy's teaching us how to squeeze orange juice."

Janice stopped in her tracks. Squeeze orange juice? Hesitantly she approached the sounds of enthusiastic domesticity coming from the boys. "Oh," she moaned, looking at the orange pulp spilling over the sides of the juicer and the half ounce of juice that had reached the pitcher.

"Where's your Uncle Randy?" David asked, trying to keep from laughing at the expression on Janice's face.

"He's in the kitchen. He's cooking the bacon," Jason said brightly. "Are you staying for breakfast? We'll make extra juice."

"We'll see," David said, turning away before he exploded with laughter. Janice began mopping up the spillage as she showed the boys how to empty the juicer into the pitcher.

Randy was leaning against the sink, pretending to watch the bacon. His eyes were closed, and he clutched a glass of Alka-Seltzer in both hands. The bacon was on the verge of charring as David removed it from the heat.

"I guess I don't have to ask how you're doing today," David said as he put the bacon on a paper towel to drain. "Why don't you get some coffee and sit down. Breakfast will be ready in about fifteen minutes."

Whistling cheerfully as he worked, David started more bacon, broke and mixed eggs and began to stack a tray with plates, silverware and butter.

Randy grumbled as he blearily served himself coffee and contemplated the leaden skies. "What a day. Looks just the way I feel," he groaned.

"I just hope last night was worth it," David said with a grin as he poured the eggs into the heated skillet and stirred them. "Send in the boys. It's time to set the table."

Randy slouched from the kitchen, and a moment later a curious Janice appeared. "Oh, you don't have to do that, David," she said, startled.

"I'm enjoying it," he replied, dropping bread into the toaster. "Here," he added, handing her a knife, "why don't you butter the toast while I finish cooking."

Janice waited, knife in hand, while the toaster glowed red. Perhaps it was her exhaustion, or perhaps it was the gray sky, but Janice felt totally relaxed as she stood at the counter waiting for the toast. David was efficiently turning the eggs out onto a platter, a towel tied around his waist, as the last batch of bacon sizzled on the grill. The overhead lights were on, and his dark hair threw back auburn glints as he moved. His tie was draped over a chair back along with his suit jacket, and his shirtsleeves were rolled up to the elbows, his collar unbuttoned. He looked absorbed in what he was doing. A small smile played around his lips, and he looked right at home in front of her stove in the large old-fashioned kitchen.

As she buttered the hot toast and placed it on a growing pile folded in a dish towel, Janice watched him. This one moment, she realized in astonishment, was just perfect. The weather, the man whistling and fussing over breakfast, her own tired acceptance of the day, all combined to produce a tranquil happiness different from anything she could remember feeling.

Finally breakfast was ready, and they carried the trays to the porch where they found Randy dozing in the corner chair and the boys intently poring over a bird book.

During breakfast, David and the boys discussed the habits of the catbird, a relative of the mockingbird, whose call came loudly from the bushes at the corner of the house. "Doesn't he sound like a cat?" Jonathan insisted. "There are two of them."

"They've got a nest in the bamboo," Jason eagerly contributed. "I saw it yesterday. It's too high to see into, and they didn't like me getting close, anyway."

"They've probably got babies. Catbirds are very protective of their young," David said.

"Really?" Randy's eyes were wide awake, the shadows gone from his face. "What are the little gray birds with the crests? I've seen a whole bunch of them around here lately."

"Titmice," Jason proudly shouted. He giggled, "They like peanuts."

"They're in the book," Jonathan added. "David told us about them. He's got lots at the horse farm. Even owls." His voice lowered with awe. "They're mean. David says they eat mice, but we've never seen that," he added.

"So you're a bird expert," Randy said, turning to David.

"Oh, yes," Janice's soft voice broke in. "David is an avid bird-watcher. He's taken us on hikes in the hills to see them."

"Good," Randy exclaimed. "Then you can show us how to build a birdhouse. The boys made me promise to help them, and I don't know the first thing about making one."

David laughed. "What kind of bird are you making it for?" he asked.

"Does it matter?" Randy asked, surprised.

"Of course!" David exclaimed. "You wouldn't expect a wren to live in a great, drafty starling house, would you?"

By the time Janice had cleared away the breakfast dishes and put on more coffee, Randy, David and the two boys were happily measuring, sawing and hammering nails into three different birdhouses. Excited voices rang through the house. Janice wondered how she would ever be able to stand the silence when Randy left and David no longer visited so often.

The front door closed on a gust of wind as Elaine came dripping into the hall. "Anyone home?" she yelled.

"In the kitchen," Janice called.

Elaine appeared in the doorway dramatically—her hair, usually so well kempt, hung in wet strands over her forehead and cheeks. Her neat slacks were drenched halfway up her calves, and the cuffs were saturated with red mud. She was barefoot, and her wet shirt was plastered against her thin body. "Look at me," she demanded. "Have you ever seen such a sight!"

"What happened to you?" Janice asked, horrified. "Go upstairs right now and take a shower. I'll get some dry clothes."

For once in her life, Elaine took orders, allowing Janice to usher her up the stairs and into the bathroom. "I forgot. I left the car here this morning. There's never enough space to park down there when the contractors are working." As she took off her wet clothing, she called through the door, "I just couldn't wait to tell you. The nursery is complete! We can start putting the plants in right away! Only another week or so for the rest, but we've still got plenty to do until then, and anyway—"

The shower cut off her excited voice in midstream. Janice chose a soft, dry jogging suit for Elaine, leaving it over a chair in the bedroom before she went back downstairs.

Janice hugged the news to herself, grinning as she poured herself fresh coffee. Done! Tomorrow afternoon she could restock and start new cuttings. Some of the plants she'd stored in the warehouse at Chantilly were still alive, and now she could bring them home and care for them properly.

Her fingers itched to be at work on her magical indoor world. She leaned against the counter, looking out at the dark, low storm clouds hugging the horizon as she dreamed of walking through the lush tropical warmth of the fragile glass-enclosed garden.

Chapter Nine

Janice cranked the red-and-white-striped canvas awning out over the flagstone patio and checked the sky to the west. So far, so good. It was actually one of the nicest days of the summer. The sky was a deep cerulean blue, even this early in the morning when the last pink flush of dawn was still fading from the eastern sky. She hoped fervently that the rest of the day would live up to this morning's promise. If it started to rain, or if the humidity climbed too high, even the awnings wouldn't attract enough people to make the opening of the garden center a success.

Most of the work had already been done. The boys had spent yesterday sweeping the flagstones clear of mulch and fragments of construction debris. Janice was proud of them. Yesterday had been as glorious as today promised to be, but they had diligently stuck to their task, taking as much care with the slate slabs edged by pine bark mulch as they did with their horses. Young faces intent, they'd dusted and scrubbed the stones until they'd almost shone. And then, rather than running off to escape further chores, they'd placed themselves at David's side and fetched and carried for the rest of the afternoon with never a complaint.

She shook her head, remembering. How did he do it? Let her try to get the boys involved in such a project—she would succeed, of course, but she'd end up exhausted from the effort needed to keep them at the task. With David, they'd volunteered. She wondered how they'd have been with Jay. Even the few years that he'd had with them had been spent at the hospital, his offices or with his nose in a medical journal. He'd been so busy building up a practice that he'd missed seeing just how fast his sons were growing. She'd been the one who'd told him what the boys had said that was amusing, or what they'd done in school that day. Would they ever know how much their father had loved them? At the time it hadn't seemed so important to tell them—Jay had expected a lifetime in which to do so.

Poor Jay. Just two years, but she felt as though she'd finally left him behind. There was so little of him left in her life, now that the house he'd bought was gone. In her memories, Jay was the tall, older and effective person she'd met and married, but she'd changed since then. If she were to meet him now, she wondered, would he still seem that way? She suspected that she'd at least be on equal ground now. No longer could she see herself as the naive, unformed girl who'd had his children and kept his house. She'd learned so much in these two years, matured of necessity, that sometimes she didn't even recognize herself.

When she tried to visualize Jay, these days, his form was blurred, his dark hair still curled vigorously just as the boys' did, but his face was in shadow. The one thing that most shocked her when she looked at pictures of him was how young he now seemed, younger even than Randy.

Standing there in the morning breeze, Janice looked around proudly at the nursery and its grounds. All the underbrush had been cleared away from the old barn, and newly planted shrubs marked the line between the business and the rest of her property. The drive that wound between century-old oak trees had been graded and covered with gravel. The parking lot and entrance to the garden center were right at the corner of the highway and the lane that continued past the house's driveway, so that customers would not be likely to stray too near her house. That had been Randy's idea, and its execution had been surprisingly simple.

Open to a view from the highway, the bright awnings of the nursery acted as a flag for passing motorists. Janice had used the same sign she'd made for the first garden center, and the bright red cardinals looked even better here, surrounded by rolling countryside. The former barn was now bright and attractive. The weather-beaten stones, fallen into piles when the old structure had collapsed, had been reused, and Janice loved the mottled effect of the moss-stained surfaces in conjunction with the many windows.

In fact, she reflected, the best thing that had happened to her recently had been the discovery of the old Indian burial ground. That, which had seemed such a tragedy at the time, was now shown to be a blessing. And not only for the business, she thought, catching a glimpse of herself in the windows. As always, even a passing thought of David made her heart race and cheeks flush, and she felt like a young girl in love. But, she reminded herself, she was no longer young, and perhaps had no right to feel so giddy. The self-admonition made no difference. A silly smile remained on her face even as she raised the blinds and unlocked the doors. If her old customers came, and the newspaper ads did their work, this first officially open day at the new address would be a day to remember.

A familiar straw-colored van turned into the lot.

"Mr. Porter!" Janice called from the door. She hurried over to the van.

A cheerful bearded face, followed by a slight, wiry body, climbed down and slid open the side door. "You sure know how to pick 'em," he said, winking. "Won't be muggy either," he added, expertly casting a glance at the southwestern sky. He handed down a dolly, and Janice stacked boxes of ceramic flowerpots and saucers as he passed them to her. "Emile's right behind me," he said as he took the dolly and trundled his wares over to the patio. "Hmm," he said looking around. "Nice spot you've got here. Right on the main road." He picked the best corner for himself. "I'll put my stuff here, and Emile can go next to me. He's bringing some of his birdbaths. Hope you've got enough room for him." When she nodded, he turned, unfolded a table and shelves and began arranging his pots.

The day had begun. Emile pulled up in his pickup truck. Right behind him, Mrs. Cable arrived with a trunkful of macramé hanging plant holders. With no fuss and remarkable efficiency, she slung a hammock, two hanging chairs and all of her wares from every available rafter and tree limb in the area. Shortly thereafter, everyone had arrived and set up shop.

Janice looked frantically around for Elaine. She hadn't realized there were going to be this many people. The local vineyard, recommended by David, had cases of Virginia wines stacked under the shade of the colorful awning. Mr. Porter had set up his potter's wheel and was cheerfully working a lump of clay prior to throwing it. Emile, it turned out, was almost a carbon copy of his brother, with the same bearded grin and slight frame. His birdbaths, however, were fantastical renderings of woodland creatures with upraised paws, and gigantic plants with cupped leaves. The raw concrete they were formed from looked great, though, against the dark vegetation where they were placed. Janice wondered if Emile made a reasonable living from these creations.

Mr. Macdougal, whose Scottish descent was not readily apparent, and whose looks came more from his Oriental mother, had arrived with a truckload of the miniature plants whose training and forming were his specialty. The bonsai pines, yews and junipers, among others, stood in the shade of large Japanese paper umbrellas he'd set up at one end of the patio.

Mr. Macdougal's wife, Irene, sat beside her husband, easel turned for the best light, paints opened and ready. She had interspersed her delicate paintings of wildflowers, roses and insects with her husband's bonsai, and the two of them made an old-fashioned picture of the eccentric couple as they went about their business oblivious to their surroundings.

Elaine finally appeared, just when Janice had given up on her nerves and begun to enjoy the confusion. "Janice," she called as she walked over from the car. "How is everything going? It looks great." She deposited a large bag at the door. "Sorry I took so long, but at the last minute the phone rang, and I couldn't get away." She glanced around shrewdly and drew her partner over to the person she'd driven up with. "Janice, this is Rebeccah. She and her husband run the Near East Delicatessen I told you about. He's bringing the food, and Rebeccah is seeing to the tables."

The two women shook hands, and Rebeccah murmured her congratulations for the new shop. The stocky middle-aged woman had a soft young voice that was shockingly at odds with her looks, but her smile was as fresh and innocent as that of a child.

Elaine's very presence seemed to lower the hectic pace of the morning, and Janice was able to get a cup of coffee and sit down to rest her feet. The worry that had nagged at her all morning now crystallized—David hadn't shown up yet. She didn't know whether to feel anxious or slighted.

She found herself watching the road as she sipped her coffee. The fear she'd had that Randy's return to Saudi Arabia would spell an end to David's visits had proved unfounded. If anything, he seemed to be around more often. However, since her part in Riverbend had been completed, she'd missed him. She hadn't realized how much the knowledge of his proximity had meant to her. Now her days seemed lonely, whether she was with Elaine, the boys or any of her other friends. No one seemed to be able to fill the spot that David did.

At eleven o'clock the first customer drove in, and by eleven thirty the parking lot was filling up. Mr. Porter and the Macdougals were throwing themselves wholeheartedly into their demonstrations, and both tables were at the center of a milling group of interested customers. The potter's wheel was spinning off vases, jars and flowerpots under Mr. Porter's skilled hands, to a continuous, enthusiastic description of each and every step in the process. His finished works were selling quickly.

The bonsai lectures were attracting just as many people as the vases. Mr. Macdougal's booming voice rang above all others, and Janice, showing people through the greenhouse, had to hide her laughter at his medicine-show delivery. The first time she'd met him, she remembered, it had taken some time for her to realize that his extravagant style was all show. His depth of knowledge about bonsai was enormous, and since that time she'd grown to have a great respect for his ability with the little sculptured plants.

Mrs. Macdougal was quiet, not that anything she said would have carried over her husband's bellow. As she painted, she kept a sharp eye on both her own drawings and the bonsai plants, bargaining with interested buyers and keeping close track of sales and prices. All the while her nimble fingers were sketching the delicate lines of Queen Anne's lace onto a sheet of paper carefully tacked up on a drawing board. Around her, in sharp contrast to her businesslike demeanor, page after page of flowers done in pastel colors fluttered from a clothesline as they dried, and her husband's brightly colored paper umbrellas rustled above their tables.

The next time Janice had a free moment, she went outside, and there was David, brown hair gleaming in the sunlight. He was wandering among the tables with the boys in eager attendance. He looked utterly relaxed, at home in old, worn jeans and sneakers. She tried not to admit how her heart leaped at the sight of him, and instead made her way to the stand where pita sandwiches and iced tea were to be found. As hard as she tried, though, it was no use. While she bought a drink, she could sense his movements as he watched Mr. Porter and then sauntered over to listen to Mr. Macdougal.

Just as she was sure he was coming over to her, he turned away to greet a distinguished gray-haired man in a jogging suit. Janice, amused at her conceit, watched. With minimal effort, David managed to

look completely in control of the situation as he kept
the boys happy and talked with his friend. Janice
envied that ability.

How many sides were there to this man? she wondered, watching him. She'd seen him passionate,
known him as a welcome companion on rainy days,
a man unfazed by kitchen duty, and she'd seen him
cold, even ruthless in pursuit of what he wanted.
He'd become a good friend of Randy's, and his relationship with the boys was somehow that of a contemporary commanding their respect. Now he was
laughing and speaking to a dignified and obviously
successful man who was at least twenty years his
senior. Janice could see that they were talking on
equal terms, the disparity in age no impediment to
their friendship.

How infinitely complex David was, she thought,
fascinated as she watched him.

And how handsome he was: his animated features, his wide, spontaneous smile, the gestures ac-
companying his words, and those sparkling eyes
interested in everything. Time stood still, sound
faded, and Janice could see nothing but David, hear
nothing but the pounding of her heart in her ears,
feel nothing but the powerful attraction that riveted
her attention to him, to his every movement. She
sagged against the shop doorframe, unable to wrench
her fascinated gaze from him when his eyes met hers.

Involuntarily they moved toward each other, taking one step, two, before Jason saw her and ran over
calling excitedly, "Mommy, Mommy." The gray-
haired gentleman turned to David and asked, "Is this

Mrs. Haley?'' He advanced, hand extended, while David tried to collect himself, and Janice pulled herself together in time to offer a shaky smile and trembling hand.

"Janice, I'd like to introduce you to Nigel Culmore. He's an old friend..."

Janice smiled and nodded, exhilarated by the effort of conversing sensibly while her whole being was focused solely on David—his nearness, his confident power that enfolded her and made her aware of her own sexuality.

That tension and awareness of him stayed with her the rest of that day and beyond. Janice was appalled at how lonely she felt when David was called out of town the following week. She counted the days until his return, and all the while she moved as though in a dream, waiting for him—the sound of his voice, the knowledge of his presence, the touch of his hand.

A week later the phone was ringing as Janice came back up the driveway after having fetched the Sunday paper. Elaine's excited voice greeted her, "Look in the Garden section, page G-2. I'll talk to you later," she said, hanging up.

Janice put the receiver back in its cradle and took the paper out to the porch table. Spreading it with impatient fingers, she stopped at the display of pictures showing the opening of the garden center. Even in black and white, the energy of that day came across. There were the Macdougals, Mr. Porter and his brother, a rack of macramé planters, and, above all, the garden center itself, looking as beautiful as Janice herself saw it.

She sat back, a foolish grin on her face as she cherished all the memories of that day.

David's friend, Nigel Culmore, had done them proud. A retired judge, he wrote articles for many major newspapers on gardening and country living. He had met David at an Audubon Society meeting more than ten years earlier, and over those years the two had become firm friends despite the difference in their ages. His article on the E & J Garden Center emphasized the classes given in bonsai, the expert advice on ailing shrubs given by Janice and the consignments of garden-related handicrafts by local Virginians. One striking picture showed the renovated nursery building silhouetted against the Appalachians, and the caption compared its design favorably with that of other contemporary structures moving into the Virginia hills.

The rumble of gravel under tires heralded David's arrival, and upstairs the boys went into a flurry of activity, pulling on boots and gathering their riding gear together. As he came into the house, their eyes met and the familiar electricity shot through her, but he didn't even have a moment to stop for coffee before the boys hurtled downstairs, excitedly anticipating their morning's ride. With a rueful smile at Janice, David bowed to their urgency and, within five minutes of his arrival, they were gone.

Janice watched the Jeep disappear down the driveway. Ever since the previous Sunday, there had been a change in her relationship with David. Although nothing had been said—indeed Janice had barely had a chance to say hello to him—tension was building. She had the sense of something waiting to happen, gathering momentum during the busy week, as though the almost sensual feel of anticipation had taken on a life of its own and become significant in itself.

She knew something was bound to happen, but caught in this extended moment, the anticipation was, for the time, enough. Sipping her coffee, she smiled a secret smile. She could sense David's mounting impatience, but he, too, was enthralled, biding his time.

Lazily she rolled up the paper, put her cup in the sink and locked the front door. She felt a bit silly, considering she was going only to the end of the driveway, but the habit was too much for her.

It was about ten-thirty when she unlocked the business. The two high-school students she'd hired to help out for the summer would arrive at noon. By then, business should be picking up. Sunday afternoon was always the busiest time of the week, when families went out to the country for the day, stopping along the roads to search for out-of-the-way bargains.

She hummed to herself as she cut out the article and tacked it to the shop bulletin board. To think that she'd been upset with David for not showing up early at the nursery's opening last week. She stood back to survey the board. Open just a bit more than a week, she thought proudly, and already the board was filling up with notices of classes, merchandise and puppies and guppies for sale. She grinned. Wait until the boys saw that notice! Well, she wouldn't be the one to point it out to them.

Elaine arrived with sandwiches while Janice was trimming the yucca plants for cuttings. They toasted their newfound fame with a bottle of Evian water before getting back to work. The students were outside carting mulch, gravel and shrubs to customers' cars.

Before they knew it, it was four o'clock, and the shadows were beginning to lengthen. With only one hour to go, business picked up even more, and all four were kept on the run.

"Janice," Elaine called irritably. "Can you get that? I'm on the other line with Mrs. Sedgwith," she said, grimacing.

Sympathetically Janice hid a smile and picked up the phone. "E & J Garden—"

"Janice?" David interrupted her. "Listen, I'm down at the Shenandoah Doctor's Hospital and…"

"What's happened?" Janice tried to control the panic she felt rising.

"It's nothing serious," David said firmly. "Please take it easy—"

"Tell me!" Janice cried, oblivious of Elaine's now concerned face turned her way.

"Jason's broken his leg. He fell off his horse this afternoon, and the doctors are looking at him now. Can you get over here right away? They need insurance information and your release for treatment."

"I'll be right there." Janice hung up the phone and looked around blankly, her breath shuddering.

"What is it?" Elaine demanded.

"Jason's broken his leg," she said, jumping up as she spoke and fiddling with her purse and car keys. "He's at the Doctor's Hospital. I've got to go..." She left the office, Elaine's voice following her with concern.

She never knew how she made it to the hospital. The drive would always be a blank in her memory. She held the wheel with single-minded intensity, picturing her son hurt, without her.

David's presence barely registered on her. He met her at the Emergency entrance and introduced her to the doctor.

The doctor was too young, she thought, as she tried to concentrate on his words. Broken leg... concussion... stay the night... sign here...

"He's asking for you," the young man concluded as he checked her signature and ushered her into the examining room. "He's in pain." At her shocked expression, he explained. "We can't sedate him or give him anything until we know about the concussion."

Jason, her baby, lay there, white and tight-lipped against the pillows, and Janice could feel his distress as he tried to look brave.

"We're waiting for the X rays. Jason's been a brave kid," the doctor said as Janice searched for words. "Ah, here they are. Mrs. Haley, if you would look over here..." He drew her attention to the pictures. "Here's the fracture," he said, showing her the threadlike lines that crossed the bone just above the ankle. "Hmm," he said, turning to Jason. "See that? You're pretty lucky, even if you don't feel that way. Any lower and it would have been your ankle. That's hard to fix properly. Well," he said, nodding at the pictures and clicking his tongue. "Straightforward setting and cast. No problem, Mrs. Haley."

Janice felt as though her head were spinning. No problem? She looked at Jason's white face. How could they say that? And what about the concussion? As she remembered, she turned quickly to the doctor, but he was busy with the staff as they prepared to set Jason's leg.

"David," Jason whispered. "I want David."

As though he'd been waiting to be called, David came into the small room and took Jason's extended hand. "How's it going?"

"They're going to set it," Jason said, smiling bravely up into David's face. "When do you think I'll be able to ride again?"

"As soon as the doctor says so," he replied calmly. "Did I ever tell you about the time I fell from old Chester at the Virginia Hunt Show?" When Jason shook his head and winced, David put his hand on the boy's shoulder and started to talk in a low voice.

Janice felt awful, helpless and unwanted. The only use she'd been to her son was to sign forms. For comfort he'd turned to someone else.

David and Jason stopped talking as the doctor rolled the trolley to the bedside. "Ready?" he asked. "All right, first things first. What kind of cast shall we give you? Hmm. I think a nice waterproof model would be just right," he said, his jolly voice grating on Janice's nerves.

"They're a bit more expensive," he confided, "but I'm sure we can talk your mother into it."

Janice wished he'd stop talking. She hoped he was a better doctor than comedian. She looked over at David. He was playing right along with the doctor's game. He didn't even look worried. Well, why should he be? Jason was her baby, not his.

They were talking about horses as the doctor wound wet brown bandages around Jason's leg. "Six weeks, maybe a bit more. You'll be back in the saddle soon enough, young man," the doctor said. Janice felt herself blanch as she thought of her son getting onto a horse again.

"How's that?" the doctor asked as he began another roll. "The pain should be going away a bit now, hmm?"

"Better," Jason mumbled tiredly.

The doctor looked at David significantly. "I think he'll sleep tonight. We'll move him over to the ward as soon as I'm finished."

As Jason nodded off, David let go of his hand and moved over to Janice's side. "Once they get him in the ward we can go pick up Jonathan."

His tired eyes kept returning to the sleeping boy, and Janice hated him in that moment—that moment when he had remembered her younger son, and she hadn't. Jonathan. How could she have forgotten all about him? And she hadn't been around when Jason had needed her, either. She moved across to the bed and looked down on her son's exhausted little face.

Chapter Ten

Janice couldn't bring herself to leave her son until Jason was installed in a semiprivate room and asleep. As they walked from the hospital into the late summer night, David took Janice's elbow and turned her toward him.

"Are you all right?" he asked, his shadowed eyes searching her face.

She mumbled something and gently pulled her arm from his grasp, fumbling for the keys to her car.

"Why don't you let me drive?" he suggested, holding out his hand to take the keys. "I came in the ambulance," he added as she shrugged and let him have the keys.

Janice averted her eyes and walked around to the passenger side of her car, avoiding contact with him. She couldn't think; only fragments of tortured thoughts seemed to roar in her mind. Jason, her baby, had barely noticed her. He'd turned to this man, the man who was responsible for his injury! She knew, deep down, below the panic, that David wasn't responsible, but in her tired, confused, jealous state, she couldn't admit that, even to herself.

If he weren't guilty, she thought irrationally, then she must be. Her neglect of her children in favor of this man and her work had finally caught up with her—the price was too high. The well-being of her sons was paramount. Never again must she allow her attention to be distracted.

She leaned back against the bucket seat and closed her eyes, trying to close out the awareness of the man next to her that filled her mind and made the car seem too close. She breathed deeply from the open window, pressing herself against the door as far from him as she could get. But it was no use. The affinity she'd felt for him ever since that very first glimpse on the late news surrounded her. His physical presence next to her and the shadows of other times with him filled her mind so that she couldn't think, could only breath, her head aching from the effort to escape the turmoil inside her.

The moon had set by the time they pulled onto a gravel driveway. Darkness closed in on the car and its headlights moved alone across the pitch-black countryside stretching invisibly beneath the distant glitter of stars. Janice shivered, and David glanced over at her, aching to hold and warm her. He shifted into a lower gear, carefully negotiating the darkened drive.

"We're almost there." David wished she would say something.

She looked out the window. "Where?" she quavered. Before she could answer, she caught her breath. Outside, against the starry sky, there was a whisper of movement, a windswept rush of power, a wave of mane in the darkness. Janice peered through the night, trying to shield her eyes from the headlights. Whatever had passed was now gone.

She heard a faint whicker carried thinly on the clover scented breeze. The car rolled to a stop, and David said, "I'll bring Jonathan out. I'm sure he's sound asleep by now."

David walked across the yard. His shoulders sagged, and his usual energetic stride was tempered. Janice climbed out of the car and turned her back on the house, seething. She didn't want to see his family now. She didn't want to be seduced by their genuine kindness. In her turmoil she stared blankly out over the night-blackened fields where the horses ran. Locked into her own dark thoughts, their freedom made no impression on her.

The events of the evening had taken their toll. She seemed unfamiliar to herself. With a ruthless clarity, she saw herself as a person who had sold her motherhood for the grand idea of independence. How had it all seemed so reasonable at the time? Standing on her own two feet had seemed desirable—even necessary for the boys. What had she accomplished for them?

In the still country night she shivered as she reviewed the cost of her quest for independence. Jason lay in the hospital, and Jonathan had fallen asleep among strangers while she'd spent the afternoon in self-congratulatory satisfaction.

She'd been so proud of herself that she hadn't noticed she'd been less attentive to her children. And now the bill for her preoccupation had come due—Jason had turned to someone else for comfort.

The sound of the front door closing spun Janice around. David held Jonathan cradled in his arms. She could hardly keep herself from snatching her child away. She felt her heart pound against her ribs as she forced herself to keep back. He placed Jonathan in the passenger seat and closed the door gently.

David took his hand from the door lock and turned to Janice. She stood rigidly at the edge of darkness, her face unreadable, features etched by shadow. Her hair had been tossed by the small breezes that were blowing across the fields, bringing with them the scents of honeysuckle and muddy riverbanks.

He was stunned. She stood there aloof and yet perfect somehow. She still wore the work clothes she'd chosen this morning, and the faded jeans molded her form so that he could see her long, slender legs, those legs that had been his first warning that here was a woman to beware of. He remembered the softness of her lips the first time he'd kissed her. Desire rose in him as she continued to stand silently, the tension that had always been between them making his hands tremble.

David felt as if his entire life had been leading him to this one moment, focusing his destiny on this

woman. Helplessly he moved toward her, seeing only
her wide dark-lashed eyes fixed on his, her serious
mouth parting. She trembled as he approached, and
he smiled, suddenly sure of his words. "Janice,
love..." He took her arms, wanting to draw her into
his embrace, but she broke free with a sudden rush
of strength and backed away, her expression hard,
unrelenting.

For a moment he couldn't move—couldn't believe what he was seeing. Impossible! He shook
himself, his hands suddenly cold with panic. What
was the matter? He'd never seen her so unapproach-
able.

He grabbed at her hand, trapping it in his own.
"What is it?"

"Nothing," she said, her voice stony. "Leave me
alone."

Frantic, he grasped her shoulders, ignoring her
attempts to pull away. "Wait, you can't go like this.
We have to talk..."

He crushed her against his chest as if the sheer
force of his own love could break through her icy
barrier. "You mean more to me than anyone ever
has. I love you," he said, holding her tightly. "Ever
since I first saw you I've known we were right for
each other—and you knew it, too. You can't deny
it!"

He loosened his grip, raising her face to meet his.
"You can't deny that we belong together. That night
at your house, that kiss we shared—you felt it as
well." His fierce gaze searched hers for an answer-

ing passion. "We're meant for each other. You know it as well as I."

David felt himself collapse inside as she twisted out of his grip, her silken hair brushing across her face, hiding her agonized expression. "Marry me," he said urgently, trying desperately to hold on to her. "We'll be happy, I promise you," he said, bracing himself against the pain as she walked away from him.

When she had the door opened, her quiet, trembling voice sank into his consciousness. "Leave me alone, David. Just stay away from us!"

He watched as she closed the car door. Red taillights inched their way down the driveway, receding with the dim glow of trees picked out by retreating headlights as she drove slowly down the gravel lane and out of his sight.

After a long time, he turned and walked slowly to the house.

Janice awoke early with tears on her cheeks. She felt bereft. Her memory of the previous night was sharp and pitilessly clear. David . . .

She moaned, turning her head into the pillow to cry. She couldn't seem to stop once she'd started. All the sobs she'd stored up for years seemed to be released now. Her slender body was racked with the violence of her emotions. Would she ever see him again?

How she had made it back home, she'd never know. Jonathan had slept peacefully as she'd inched her way through the darkness, the road ahead blurred by the first of her tears. Somehow she'd carried the sleeping child upstairs and tucked him securely into his own bed before collapsing herself.

David's stricken expression had haunted her during the night, whether awake or asleep. Her dreams had blended with her waking misery so that she was no longer sure whether she'd slept at all.

The anger had drained away, taking with it the strength it had lent her to stand aloof from his ardent pleas.

"Janice! Why haven't you answered the phone? I've been frantic!" Elaine stood in the bedroom doorway. "Do you know you left your front door unlocked last night—anyone could have walked right in." Her voice trailed off as she took in the distraught, shaking form of her friend. "Janice? What's happened?" She sat on the edge of the bed. "Is...is Jason...is Jason all right?"

Much to her surprise, Janice's tears redoubled, and she blindly flung herself into Elaine's arms. "David," she gasped with a sob. "I..." Her voice broke, and she began to shake again.

Elaine, puzzled and appalled at Janice's unbridled emotion, made comforting noises and settled herself to ride out the storm.

Janice's sobs began to die away, and not too long afterward, with an abashed shrug, she hugged her friend. "Thanks, Elaine." She sat back and swung her legs to the floor. With a wry attempt at a smile, she stood up and reached for a robe. "Sorry for being such an idiot," she said as she headed for the shower. "Would you be an angel and make some coffee?'' Her tear-swollen eyes met the anxious gaze of her friend. ''I'll be down in a minute.''

Elaine watched her disappear into the bathroom and then, deep in thought, she made her way downstairs to the kitchen. The routine of putting on the coffee kept her hands occupied. Something to do with David, Elaine thought, frowning as she measured the coffee. What could have happened?

She'd watched the two of them circling each other warily for months. Their initial attraction had been obvious from the very first moment they'd met. She laughed silently, remembering David with his nose pressed against the greenhouse window staring at Janice, and the blush with which he'd been discovered. The electricity flowing between them had sparked at their first handshake and had never dissipated.

In all her years—and Elaine readily acknowledged each and every one of them—she'd never seen anything like it. She hadn't even believed it could really exist. As a teenager, of course, she'd read the stories of the great romances: Anthony and Cleopatra, Romeo and Juliet, Elizabeth and Robert Browning. They'd been lovely, but somehow the emotions had seemed too poetic to be real.

In David and Janice, she'd come to see with a shock that such deep, true love could actually exist. At first she'd been amazed, slightly disbelieving. Later, when her initial assessment had been confirmed by their continued fascination with each other, she'd watched their maneuverings with increasing and affectionate amusement.

How could they not see what they meant to each other?

Elaine went through the house pulling back curtains and opening windows. She heard Janice get out of the shower as she got out the coffee mugs. By the time the tray was ready and on the porch, Janice's footsteps had reached Jonathan's room, stopped there for a moment and started down the stairs.

"Out here," she called.

Janice looked infinitely better. The emotional and physical exhaustion that had followed her outburst still left traces, but her hair gleamed wetly in the morning light, and her skin was rosy fresh from the shower's heat.

She smiled rather sheepishly, and Elaine was grateful that her friend's customary composure had returned.

Janice poured herself coffee.

Elaine took a deep breath and glanced at Janice assessingly. Well, she thought, the best way to deal with something is to meet it head-on. She plunged right in. "Okay, what's going on? And don't try to tell me it's nothing!" she warned.

Janice looked almost grateful for Elaine's directness. As she began to talk, she realized just how much she'd needed to. "I don't know why I haven't spoken to you before," she said. "I guess I thought if I just ignored my confusion it would go away."

Once she started talking she couldn't stop. She recounted everything that had happened over the past months: her first earth-shattering glimpse of him, their meeting, even that magical night in the garden.

She spoke reminiscently, as if of times long since gone, loves long since lost.

Underlying her friend's gently regretful voice, Elaine saw Janice's love for David shine forth like a beacon in the night. And as a counterpoint to her friend's narration, Elaine also heard the self-doubt, the suppressed yearning for an eternal love, which she couldn't believe could ever be hers.

"I feel like such a fool!" Janice's voice rose, and her eyes glistened for a moment before she steadied herself and continued. "I keep telling myself to remember I'm a mother first and foremost, and yet after each mistake, after each reminder, I do the same thing all over again."

Her eyes strayed to the ceiling, as though to see through to the room above, where her son lay sleeping. "I've been neglecting them so much—for no reason other than my own convenience. I wasn't even there when he fell from that horse."

Elaine stirred in protest. "You can't be with them all the time, Janice. They're growing up."

Janice's haunted eyes looked up at her as she whispered her private nightmare, "He could have been killed."

"But he wasn't!" Elaine said firmly, her tone brooking no argument. "That kind of thinking is useless. Anyway, you'd have to lock them up to keep them from harm, and you know it."

"You're right," Janice whispered into her hands. Then, sitting up, she said more strongly, "You're right." Thoughtfully Janice mused aloud. "I don't know what's happened to me lately. I used to think I was in control of my life, but not anymore. I don't know where I'm going, or what I'm doing. Half the time I just seem to be reacting to someone else..."

Elaine had to work hard to suppress a smile at these last words. Poor Janice. She was well and truly smitten, and she didn't even seem to realize it.

Shaking her head, she encouraged Janice to continue. "We all go through times like that, Janice."

Her friend looked over at her rather skeptically. "Yes," Elaine said, nodding, "even me." She added archly, "But that was a long time ago."

Janice gave her a wan smile and looked away, her eyes fixing on some interior memory.

"What happened?" Elaine asked gently, and Janice's eyes filled with tears.

"Jason barely noticed me. He asked for David." She looked so young, Elaine thought, helpless and lost. "He didn't need me at all. David was all he wanted. David, David, David! I never want to hear his name again!"

Elaine shook her head, looking at Janice in disbelief as the diatribe against David continued.

"He asked me to marry him! Do you believe that? Marry him," she gasped. "I told him to keep away from me, but now I don't know what to do. I don't know what I want!" She seemed to run out of breath and gazed at Elaine with wide, appalled eyes.

Both women were startled out of their concentration as a small bundle of energy burst into their midst. "Mommy, where's Jason? I want Jason!" Jonathan flung himself into his mother's arms.

Janice held her son tightly.

"Jason's quite all right, Jonathan," Elaine interjected. "He had to stay in the hospital overnight."

"I gave him a call this morning, honey." Janice rumpled her son's hair and straightened his shirt. "He's feeling just fine, but he probably won't be home until tonight or tomorrow." Jonathan squirmed out of her arms, reassured.

"I'm hungry," he said insistently, all thoughts of Jason put aside for the moment.

Janice stood up. "Come on, I'll get your breakfast." She took his hand and looked at Elaine. "Would you like more coffee?"

Elaine nodded. She sat deep in thought while Janice and Jonathan hunted up breakfast.

The back door slammed, and Elaine looked up. Janice was coming back with a full pot of coffee and a plate of croissants. "Thought you might want something to munch on," she explained.

Janice avoided Elaine's eyes as she sat down and passed the plate to her friend. She fussed with the coffee, pouring, then adding cream, sugar, placing napkins, until Elaine burst out, "Oh, for heaven's sake, will you please sit still!"

Startled, Janice looked up, her fingers suddenly crumpling the napkin she'd been unconsciously folding and refolding.

Elaine carefully put her cup down, braced herself and then, with characteristic bluntness, said, "Janice, you're my best friend, but you're a fool. Look at all the excuses you've lined up for yourself."

Janice sat back, watching Elaine with incredulous hurt in her wide eyes.

"Don't look at me like that," Elaine said, her voice gruff with swallowed emotion. "You've gone through incredible contortions to keep yourself from seeing yourself and David clearly.

"Do you have any idea how transparent you are sometimes?" Elaine asked. She continued without a pause, "I've seen through the two of you from the beginning. You should have seen David when he first caught sight of you in the greenhouse that day he came to the shop." She giggled nervously as she looked at Janice's stricken face. "He was like a boy at the window of a pet store. He kept steaming up the space he'd rubbed in the glass. He couldn't take his eyes off you."

Janice turned sharply away. David... She felt awed to learn that he too had been fascinated by the distant image of a stranger.

"And when you two shook hands—did you actually hear anything I was saying at the time? It sure didn't look it. In fact, both of you looked as though you'd been stunned, struck by lightning." She grimaced in an attempt at humor. "How else do you think I got such a deal from him?"

Elaine leaned over and, with a shaky hand, picked up her coffee cup and took a sip. She frowned. It was cold. Placing the cup beside her again, she took a deep breath and continued, "There was one point when I thought you had it all worked out. You remember the day he brought the garden center plans over?

"Before you came down he was happier than I'd ever seen him. He couldn't sit still. He was so excited about the plans—he told me he'd been working all night on them—but he refused to show them to me. He just kept chuckling under his breath, clutching those blueprints and listening for your footsteps. The moment you started downstairs, he spread them out, grinning like a Cheshire cat.'' She sat silently for a moment, remembering that morning. ''From the moment you came into the room, something went wrong,'' she continued. ''And when I came back from answering the door, the two of you were practically in opposite corners barely glancing at each other.''

How well Janice remembered! She hadn't known if she'd wanted to see him, or if she couldn't stand the sight of him. She'd been so mixed up... She realized now, listening to Elaine, that she'd barely even seen David because she'd been so wrapped up in her own conflicting emotions.

Elaine looked unusually uncomfortable. She avoided Janice's eyes as she began to speak again. ''Look, Janice, you know I'm your friend. I've been your friend for a long time now, and I want you to remember that. But I can't say I've liked the way I've seen you treat David.

''From what I've seen, he's been unfailingly kind to you. I know that I'm speaking from the outside, and if I'm wrong, tell me. But never once have I seen him try to dominate you or treat you as anything less than an equal. And, if you'd been looking, you'd have seen that he's been in love with you from the moment he first laid eyes on you.'' Elaine leaned back. "And you've been in love with him, too. So why don't you just relax and let him know that?"

She felt her own tensions drain away as she watched the successive emotions play across Janice's countenance. The nagging fear that Janice wouldn't be able to accept what she was saying died away, and she relaxed in her chair.

Elaine's words were like a revelation to Janice. They found an echo in her, and as she listened to her friend the veils of confusion that had been with her ever since that first glimpse of David began to lift. What Elaine was saying was something she now realized she already knew in her heart of hearts.

Why hadn't she been able to see his love herself? Why hadn't she been able to see how much she loved him? Swept along by the new certainty that filled her, she was suddenly impatient—a sense of urgency gripped her. She had to get to him!

She cringed inside as she thought of the pain her words the night before must have caused—not only those of the previous night, but her words and actions of the past few months as well. "Elaine," she choked out, "you're right. I've got to see him, talk to him." Shuddering, she got control of herself with an effort. She took a deep breath. "Will you excuse me? I've got some phone calls to make."

Her fingers trembled as she dialed the number for Riverbend Park, but she forced herself to remain calm. As the telephone was answered at the other end, she both hoped and feared to hear his voice. "Hello... Hello, Susan, it's Janice. Is David in?"

She tried his house next, then his parents' house and finally his uncle's house. With this last call, she discovered his probable whereabouts and wrote down explicit directions to a cabin in the mountains, including elaborate descriptions of landmarks. The kindly old gentleman was obviously curious, but Janice was able to get away without explanations.

She sat for what seemed a long time, afraid—of the dangers that might lie ahead, of the possibility that she was making a big mistake, of the suddenly unknowable shape of the future—and then she called the hospital.

It was only after swinging off the highway onto a narrow mountain road that Janice began to really think about what she was doing. As she drove carefully over the rutted road that wound between long-established woodlands of tall trees, heading even higher up the deceptively gentle slopes of the Appalachians, she wondered in amazement at herself.

What was she doing?

She'd left the Janice Haley she knew far behind, in both time and space. That Janice had been contented, sure of herself and her limited life with its limited desires. Now she found herself reaching for more than she'd ever imagined might be possible— reaching for love and completion, joy such as she'd never known existed.

She carefully negotiated a tight curve and looked down, down and even farther down over the treetops. Already the valley below looked minute. Miniature fields, cows and houses were carefully arranged on the green tapestry of the Virginia summer. The day wasn't too hot yet, but a slight haze had already settled into the valley, lending an air of illusory enchantment to the pastoral scene.

Janice's spirits began to rise to match her progress upward through the hills. For the first time ever in dealing with David, she felt sure of herself. Elaine was watching Jonathan, and she'd had a long talk with Jason, who was feeling much better and would be released from the hospital later that evening. The confusion she'd been suffering from for months had untangled itself, as though it had been washed away in the clear, light-headed freedom that had come to her with Elaine's words.

Elaine had made her see what she'd known all along. If only she'd trusted her intuition. How could she have ever fooled herself into thinking that her wonderful night with David could have been anything other than true?

The car bumped and swayed over a rocky stretch, and Janice slowed even further. She'd been afraid, she knew. Afraid to trust in anyone, in anything that wasn't permanent and immortal.

She'd thought she was over Jay's death, but now she realized that she might never be. She might always have to fight the fear that those she gave her love to would leave her in one way or another—and that was irrational, she knew. The future could never be foretold, and so life must be lived fully and love must be cherished wherever it was found.

This was it!

A huge outcrop of jagged rock rose stark in the sunlight. Creepers and stringy-looking saplings fought for a toehold among its crevices. Immediately opposite, a track barely wide enough for her small car wound through grass and blackberries. David's uncle had been painstaking in his description, Janice thought as she turned down toward the place where the cabin should be.

Any calm she might have acquired during the drive deserted her utterly as she maneuvered carefully through the sudden shadow of the trees now overhead. A flash of reflected light caught her eye as it pierced the shade, and she stepped on the brakes quickly as the Jeep came around a corner right in front of her.

David! Janice's heart raced, and her hands seemed locked to the wheel.

A car door slammed, loud in the still woodlands, breaking the spell that had held her in place. She opened the door and stood up, her eyes dazzled by the dancing sunlight.

He was standing on the other side of his car, his hand on the hood. No grin today, Janice thought as her eyes focused on him. His whole stance bespoke waiting, and his eyes, those eyes that had entranced her when he'd still been a stranger, were looking at her, questioning her.

With a small, inarticulate cry, she took a step forward, her eyes searching his for her welcome, but his expression didn't change, and Janice stopped.

"Is Jason all right?" he asked in a stranger's voice.

His words cut through her sentimental conviction that all would be right with a word or gesture from her. She nodded, unable to speak. Her heart was breaking as she realized how terribly she'd hurt him last night with those harsh, unforgiving words she now wished she'd never uttered.

For the second time that day she felt the tears come, and she turned away, ashamed of her weakness. How had she made such a mess of things?

"Janice?" David's voice softened, and she felt his hands on her shoulders, felt him turn her, felt his arms wrap around her and hold her as she gulped for control. "Don't cry," he murmured against her hair. "Don't cry."

"Oh, David, I love you," she managed to say through her tears. "I never meant to hurt you. I was jealous. Jason turned to you and not to me. You were the one who was there for him, and I wasn't. But it's more than that..."

She pulled away, avoiding his eyes, and took the handkerchief he held out for her.

"Come on back to the cabin," he said as she rubbed the tears from her cheeks. "I could use some coffee—I don't know about you."

She let him start back past his Jeep, while she took a deep breath, trying to regain her composure, and then followed. The track was overgrown with bracken, and long thorny blackberry stems reached out to snag the unwary. Carefully she followed David's twisting path through the maze of growth.

The cabin stood in a small clearing right on the edge of the mountain, with the whole valley spread out below. Far in the distance, she could see the beginning of the winding road she'd traveled so short a time ago.

She walked onto the porch. David had disappeared into the cool interior, and she leaned on the rail, taking strength and courage from the fresh mountain vistas. Wings spread, two turkey buzzards circled above her, floating lazily up the mountain on the warm air rising from the valley.

By the time David came onto the porch with two mugs of hot coffee, Janice was calm and ready to face him. She felt confident, now that they were together, that all would be well.

"Oh, David," Janice sighed, putting down her mug. "I can't believe I was so mean to you last night. I was jealous, angry, afraid...and I took it all out on you.

"Ever since I first saw you, I've wanted you. And from the first moment I wanted you I've been fighting that feeling," she said.

David moved restlessly, but Janice shook her head. "Let me go on. I need to say this." She forced herself to keep looking at him. "I was afraid of falling in love, afraid of committing myself to something and then losing it, and I was afraid that, well, that you would laugh at me."

"Laugh at you?" David was astonished.

In a small, embarrassed voice she said, "Well, I am a widow with two boys, and you're a bachelor with everything you could want..."

David snorted in derision. "Everything I want!" Angrily he strode over to her and shook her slightly.

"Janice!" He shook his head again. "Janice, ever since the first time I saw you I've been obsessed with you." He glared at her look of incomprehension. "Why are you looking so amazed? Surely you could tell." Exasperated at all the frustration he'd felt because of her, yet unable to deny the desire that surged through him at her closeness, he gave her a hard kiss on the mouth.

"And you, of all people, talk about being jealous!" He laughed at the memory of his bitterness. "I almost killed Randy before I knew who he was." Janice looked at him in amazement. "That day he came to the site and whirled you around, and you looked so happy and kissed him."

She began to laugh helplessly as she remembered his strange moods and the tension of those weeks. He looked shocked for a moment but then he clasped her in his arms and held her tightly, remembering the black moods and his despair. They'd all been groundless.

Janice leaned into the warmth of his arms, feeling the rumble of his voice, "And you should have heard Jason before you got to the hospital yesterday," David said. "All he could say was 'Where's Mom?' The moment you entered the room he quieted down." He looked down at her. "So don't you ever talk about jealousy again."

Janice began to speak, looking up at him from the circle of his arms, but she said nothing. In his eyes, the love he felt for her was finally apparent, shining clear and tender now that all her own confusion and doubt had been vanquished.

Why had she resisted? Why had she fought against loving this man? She could no longer remember. It didn't matter. She loved him—heart, mind and soul. The familiar fascination he always awoke in her returned, and she felt his own passion awaken.

Their lips met, a mingling of tears and summer breeze and the slightly smoky aroma of camp coffee. They held on to each other, their kiss deepening, becoming the promise of present and future love and all time to come.

They stood, locked in each other's arms, while around them the summer sun touched the young flowers, gently opening their petals to the light.

COMING NEXT MONTH

IT TAKES A THIEF—Rita Rainville
When Dani Clayton broke into the wrong office at the wrong casino, she was caught—by devastating Rafe Sutherland. Dani was determined to get to the right place; Rafe was determined to keep her out. Two such strong-willed people just *had* to fall in love.

A PEARL BEYOND PRICE—Lucy Gordon
Not even the barriers from their pasts could prevent the sparks that flew between Renato and Lynette. Renato was a hard man—would he ever understand the pricelessness of Lynette's love?

IN HOT PURSUIT—Pepper Adams
Secret Service Agent J. P. Tucker had been trailing Maggie Ryan for weeks. But it wasn't until after he'd rescued her from kidnappers and counterfeiters, and was chased all over the state, that he realized there was more to shy Maggie than met the eye!

HIGH RIDER—Olivia Ferrell
Rodeo clown Rama Daniels wanted a stable home life, and she was sure she couldn't have one with Barc Lawson. Barc was a rodeo rider, a nomad. Though he professed he was ready to settle down, Rama knew rodeo was in his blood. Could he ever convince her otherwise?

HEARTS ON FIRE—Brenda Trent
Glenna Johnson had always wanted to be a firefighter, and now she had her chance. She knew she could put out the fires, but could she handle the burning glances of station captain Reid Shelden?

THE LEOPARD TREE—Valerie Parv
Her first UFO! Tanith had always wanted to see one, and now she had. But was the mysterious, compelling stranger who arrived with it alien or human? Evidence said alien, but her heart said he was very much a man.

AVAILABLE THIS MONTH:

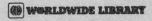